Samuel Alexander Purdie

**Memories of Angela Aguilar de Mascorro**

And sketches of the Friends' Mexican mission

Samuel Alexander Purdie

**Memories of Angela Aguilar de Mascorro**
*And sketches of the Friends' Mexican mission*

ISBN/EAN: 9783337097370

Printed in Europe, USA, Canada, Australia, Japan

Cover: Foto ©Raphael Reischuk / pixelio.de

More available books at **www.hansebooks.com**

# MEMORIES

OF

# ANGELA AGUILAR DE MASCORRO;

AND

## SKETCHES OF THE FRIENDS' MEXICAN MISSION.

By Samuel A. Purdie.

Publishing Association of Friends,

CHICAGO, ILL.

1885.

# ERRATA.

A few typographical errors have escaped the attention of the author in proof reading.

Page 81.—CHAPTER XIII should be CHAPTER XII.

The division of several words at end of lines has been accidentally erroneous.

The statement on page 48 that there were only two inquisitions in Spain in 1559. is probably an error, yet the Autos in which *Protestants* suffered were limited to Valladolid and Seville.

By the statement on page 97–"who though know under another name are really Jesuit," it is not intended to state that the "*Oblates of Mary*" are a part of the Jesuit order, but a kindred institution.

# INTRODUCTORY SKETCH.

The great liberal movement of 1857, led by Benito Juarez, gave religious liberty to Mexico and paved the way for a reform movement, & for introducing the Protestant worship into the country. Soon after two priests led forward two independent movements in this direction. That of Ramon Lozano is clearly portrayed in this volume. One in the city of Mexico initiated by a priest named Aguilar became the nucleus of the Protestant Episcopal Mission established about the year 1869 or 1870. In this latter year a Dominican Priest named Manuel Aguas read several leaflets with a view to refute the arguments of the Protestant missionaries but becoming convinced of the truth of the reasonings of his opponents he openly espoused the Protestant cause which he defended with ability and preached with an energy superior to his physical strength. In November of 1872 he was left in charge of the mission by Bishop Riley, and on one occasion fainted in the pulpit and was carried to his room where he died from the results of his over exertion.

He was an able controversial writer and his death was a severe stroke to the cause, yet just at that time the missions which had been opened in Zacatecas and Nuevo Leon by the American Christian Union began gaining strength, the Baptist churches were organized, and the Friends' Mexican Mission was opened by the writer of this volume on the 28th of November 1871.

My attention was called to this field, because having become interested in the spread of peace principles, for which I had suffered somewhat during the war which desolated my native land, I longed to do something to stay the tide of blood which was being shed in intestine strife in these countries, and to give them the Gospel of peace and purity in place of their superstitions Romanism, and the degrading influence of their priesthood.

My aim was a Publishing House, and the title of our paper, "El Ramo de Olivo," was written on a fly leaf of my Latin Lexicon, long ere I offered my services to the Friends' Foreign Mission Association of Indiana Yearly Meeting, which was in April 1871.

Just after offering my services to them I learned that a Spaniard was working in a gold mine about three miles from my home, near Ashboro N. C. and on making him a visit, being able to speak intelligibly a few words in his native tongue, this fact drew him to me in near affection. I often read with him in Spanish Tracts and on leaving for Mexico gave him my Spanish Bible.

My expectation was to locate at Victoria, capital of Tamaulipas, and if possible make the work as near self-sustaining as practicable.

At that time there were no international mail facilities between the Spanish American Republics, and it was evident that my expectations would in part be frustrated. It was providential that I was in the field with a use of the language perhaps surpassed by few foreigners and with an able corps of native contributors to the paper ere it could wing its way to those countries.

Detained in Matámoros by the Revolution which terminated with the death of Benito Juarez, a congregation had gathered around us giving promise of great local good, and it did not seem best to leave this gathering for a new field, and thus for our book work this change proved very beneficial as it placed us in the free trade belt where we could import paper free of duty, thus reducing the cost of materials to one half what it would have been at Victoria, and we could also use the facilities of the United States postal laws for remitting our publications to other Spanish Countries, thus we see the wisdom of our Heavenly Father in detaining us where we could be most extensively useful.

Our first work was tract distribution from our rooms at 64 and 66 Calle de Matamoros, and we were abundantly supplied with those issued by the American Tract Society, through the kind influence of our friend Robert Lindley Murray, and through the kindness of the American Bible Society books were furnished for a vigorous canvass of the city, where over 500 Bibles and Testaments were circulated through our agency during the year 1872. Often in after years on interrogating a new convert, either in our own or the Presbyterian Mission, they would refer to books which they had received through our canvassers, who received a small compensation from sales, but never hesitated to give when it seemed best.

In the summer of 1872 our Friend Anna C. Tatum of New York and her two sisters gave us a Small Quarto Cottage press and 75 lbs. of type, in order to issue tracts setting forth more particularly those important points of Gospel Truth which seemed partially to be overlooked by other churches, among these Peace Tracts being particularly necessary.

We at once issued our monthly paper, "El Ramo de Olivo," which has been continued to the present time with a constantly enlarging field of influence in the cause of Christ.

The want of suitable school books for our Mission Schools was apparent so soon as they were established, which was early in

1872. The School Books issued in Mexico were intensely Catholic, those issued in New York by business firms though less so, all had Catholic forms of prayer, whilst those from Paris were more or less antagonistic to all religion.

We had to begin with A. B. C. although our First Reader was better adapted to the word method than any other book which had preceded it. We only hoped to supply *our own school* and 144 copies were issued. This edition lasted over two years and was mostly circulated gratuitously. Just as it was exhausted in 1874, Presbyterian and Methodist Missions were organized in all parts of the country and our "First Reader" was called for. From that time to the present it has gained favor until about 1000 copies per month are sold to schools in Mexico, Texas and New Mexico. It has been followed by a complete series of reading books, decidedly evangelical in their teaching, and unexpectedly to us they have gained favor in many public schools in all parts of Mexico.

As early as 1875 the Catholic Papers declared our Juvenile Issues to be the most dangerous element they had to encounter, and unless they could be counteracted the coming generation would entirely abandon Romanism.

The local work consisted of a Girls' School, and a meeting and Sabbath School, at the time the reader is introduced to the Mission in this volume, which gives a few characteristic incidents rather than a detailed narrative of the work. Our work has grown up at the same time with the many other missions which have been opened in this land and to whom we feel bound as brethren in a common cause.

An inside view of Mission Work and particularly that of the Friends' Mexican Mission is given in the present volume, not with any view to claim for ourselves any growth which an increase-giving God has granted to our mission, but with thankfulness to recognize his many mercies and kind providences and the fulfilment of his promise, "Lo I am with you alway, even unto the end of the world."

SAMUEL A. PURDIE.

Matamoros, December 1. 1884.

# THE LORD'S PRAYER IN SPANISH.

## PADRE NUESTRO.

Padre Nuestro que estás en los cielos: sea santificado tu nombre; venga tu reino, sea hecha tu voluntad, como en el cielo, así tambien en la tierra: Dános hoy nuestro pan cotidiano, y perdónanos nuestras deudas, como tambien nosotros perdonamos á nuestros deudores. Y no nos metas en tentacion, mas líbranos de mal; porque tuyo es el reino, y el poder y la gloria por todos los siglos. Amen.

## THE LORD'S PRAYER IN AZTEC.

## IZCATQUI IN TOTATZINÉ.

Totatziné, inilhuicac timetztica, mayectenehualo in motocatzin: matohuicpa huala in motlatocayotzin: machlhualo in tlalticpac in motlanequilitzin, inyuh chihualo in ilhuicac. Ma axcan maxitechmomaquili, in totlaxcal momoztla yé totech monequi, ihuan maxitechmotlapopolhuili in totlatlacol, inyuhqui tiquin tlapopolhuia in tlatlacame tech tlallacalhuia: yhuan macamo xitech mo cahuili tihuetzizque ipan inteneyecoltilizpan: mazanye xitechmomaquixtili inpan nochin tlen ahmo cuali. Mayuhqui mochihua.

# TABLE OF CONTENTS.

## CHAPTER I.

## CHAPTER II.

## CHAPTER III.

## CHAPTER IV.

## CHAPTER V.

## CHAPTER VI.

## CHAPTER VII.

## CHAPTER VIII.

IX

# POSITION OF PLATES AND MAPS.

# THE SPANISH AMERICAN MISSION FIELD.

Aside from Mexico there are in *Septentrional America*, as the Spanish Geographers call that portion between the Rio Grande and the Isthmus of Darien, five other republics having similar governments to that of Mexico and in all of them the same conflict between Church and State exists as in Mexico. In Guatemala there is a powerful ANTI-CLERICAL LEAGUE, and a most resolute opposition to all clerical influence in government matters is everywhere manifest. Education is carried forward vigorously in all the principal cities, the leading female teachers being from France and tinctured with infidelity. Our papers are extensively circulated in all these republics and the public libraries are supplied with complete sets of our past volumes, and also copies of all our religious publications.

Costa Rica has but recently opened her doors to the Gospel, and the Jesuits who had charge of education have been expelled. Recently the Codifying Committee of Congress met and the leader thereof said:—"We live in the last half of the nineteenth century, and in accordance with its tenor I refuse to *administer an oath* and shall accept your promise. The Quakers were allowed this privilege two centuries ago and not a case of false evidence can be charged against them."

Regular Mail Steamship lines connect the northern ports of Central America with Veracruz, New Orleans and St. Thomas, W. I. where connecting lines run to Panamá, and La Guayra, Venezuela. There is another Mail Line, (from San Francisco to Panamá,) carrying Mexican Mails from Acapulco, touching at all the Pacific Ports.

In Colombia, Chili, Argentine Republic and Uruguay are Protestant missions, and Dr. Taylor's self-sustaining missions exist in Perú aside from a few other points. Ecuador is now closed against Protestants, and in alliance with the Jesuits who have charge of Public Instruction. Our own publications are extensively circulated outside of Protestant Mission circles in Colombia, Venezuela, Uruguay, Argentine Republic and Chili, and a few copies in Ecuador during the dictator-ship of Gen. Veintemilla. Except in Uruguay, Argentine Republic and Chili the Protestant missions have labored with but little fruit, in some places seventeen years without a convert, yet their labor is not lost, and the word of the Lord will not return unto him void, but will fulfil its purpose in His own time.

# PRONUNCIATION OF SPANISH NAMES.

As many Spanish names occur in this volume we will give a few rules for their pronunciation, which may serve as fully, *if observed*, as a vocabulary.

## VOWEL SOUNDS.

**A** is always open Italian *a* as in *father*.
**E** always has the sound of *a* in *fate*.
**I** always sounds like *ee* in *meet*.
**O** always sounds like long *o* in *pore*.
**U** always sounds like *oo* in *boot*.
**Y** when a vowel sounds like *ee* in *meet*.

## NO LETTER IS EVER SILENT EXCEPT *H*.

**B** has the same sound as in English.
**C** sounds like *k* except before *e* and *i* when it sounds like *s* in *see*.
**Ch** is a separate letter and sounds like *ch* in *church*.
**D** has the same sound as in English.
**F** same sound as in English.
**G** before *e* and *i* sounds like forcibly aspirated *h* in *high*, *here*, but in all other places it has the hard sound in English.
**H** is always silent.
**J** always has the forcibly aspirated sound of *h* as in *house*.
**L** same sound as in English.
**Ll** is a separate letter, and in Spain is sounded like *lli* in *million*, but in Mexico it is sounded like *y* in *yes*.
**M** same sound as in English.
**N** same sound as in English.
**Ñ** sound like *ny* in *canyon*.
**P** same sound as in English.
**Q** same sound as in English, and is always followed by *u*, which is not sounded before *e* unless marked *ü*, the same occurs when *u* follows *g* before *e*.
**R** has a soft sound, except when at the beginning of a word.
**Rr** is a separate letter and has a rolled trilling sound, as *r* in *forgot* is pronounced by the Scotch peasants, but a little more trilled, and foreigners rarely pronounce it correctly.
**S** always sounds soft as in *see*.
**T, V, X** and **Y** have the same sound as in English.
**Z** in Spain is sounded like *th* in *thin* but in Mexico like *s* in *see*.

## EXAMPLES.

Luciano *(loo—see—áh—know)*
Mascorro *(mahs—koe—rrho)*
Motecuhzoma *(mo—tay—koo—so—mah)*
Angelita *(ahn—hay—lee—tah.)*
Revilla-Gigedo *(Ray—vee—yah—He—hay—doe.)*
The accent is on the last syllable when ending in a consonant and on the penult when ending in a vowel. In all other cases the accent is marked. XI

# A FEW WORDS. ABOUT MEXICO.

Mexico is a country embracing a territory about equal to that portion of the United States lying east of the Mississippi River.

It is however broken by the chain of the Rocky Mountains which diversify it with fertile valleys, broad table lands, and bold rugged and barren mountain sides, with a few points capped with eternal snow.

It is a Federal Republic, similar in plan to that of the United States, and is divided into 28 States, one territory and the Federal District. On the accompanying Map the States of Tlaxcalla and Aguascalientes are printed in small letters, as they are small states like Rhode Island and Connecticut. Tepic has been declared a state in the present year 1884.

The population of 10.000.000 souls is chiefly concentrated in the central portion of the Republic, whilst the great states of the North West, are largely desert and except a few trading centres but sparsely populated.

Of this population 5.000.000 are descendants of the native races, and about 1.500.000 still speak the native languages, of which more then ten are still in use.

The Mexican or Aztec language is now taught in some of the Colleges of Puebla, Mexico and Guadalajara, and recent improved text books, whilst making the language accessible to interested persons, are contributing to educate these masses and thus Spanish will soon supplant the native tongues.

The remaining half of the population are chiefly of the mixed race so that less than one fifth of the inhabitants can be set down as of the Caucasian race.

Education is compulsory in the cities but the grade of study is generally very low and the teaching very superficial.

Its political wars have mainly been upon the question, Church and State v. s. Religious Liberty. The latter is the banner of the Liberal party, who gained the power in 1857, being led by a pure descendant of the Aztec race, Benito Juarez. The "Conservative" or Church Party aided by Napoleon III, partially regained power under the transient empire of Maximilian, but fell completely in 1867.

The confiscation of Convents and the suppression of religious orders, as well as the banishment of the Jesuits, and in 1874 of the Sisters of Charity, show that the masses can never be reconciled to Romanism, and unless the Gospel is preached must fall into an infidelity as terrible as that of the French Revolution of 1793.

The Evangelical School Books issued by Friends' Mexican Mission aside from being adopted in many public schools, are sold in most cities, and have been largely useful in counteracting unbelief and superstition, and teaching the plan of Salvation through Christ as the one Mediator.

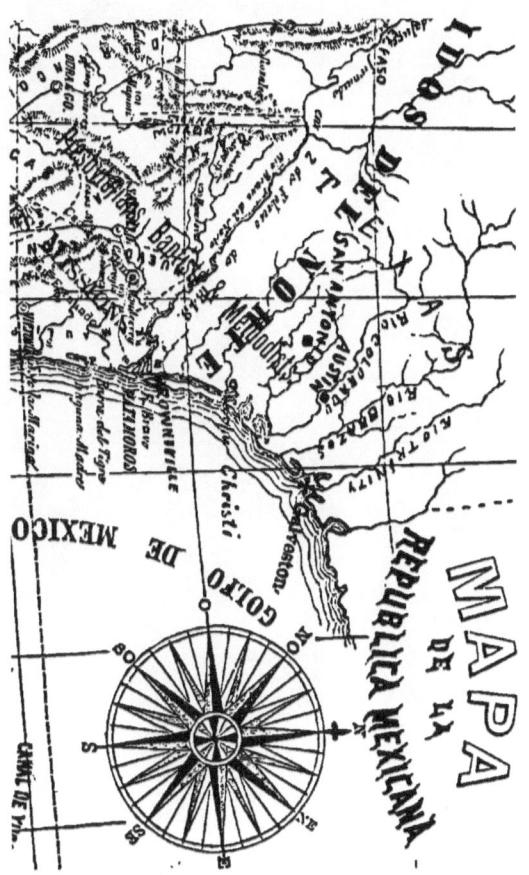

# MEMORIES OF ANGELA AGUILAR DE MASCORRO;

### AND

### SKETCHES OF THE FRIENDS' MEXICAN MISSION.

## CHAPTER I.

COMPARATIVE POSITION AND INFLUENCE OF WOMAN IN ENGLAND, THE UNITED STATES AND MEXICO, ILLUSTRATED BY FAMILIAR EXAMPLES.

MANY beautiful narratives of Christian lives made sublime by acts of self-denial and obedience to the law of the Lord, have already been published, and not a few of the most interesting of these belonged to the small body of Christians known as the Friends. This is peculiarly true of Christian women, because this church opened a wide door for the ministry of females, and in this respect as a church long stood alone.

We do not intend to censure other churches for their views, from which we must candidly differ, but devoutly thank them for the able sisters whom they have given to our ranks, rather than let them work publicly in their own.

We believe that many hearts have throbbed with interest as they have read the touching autobiography of Jane Hoskens, who, closely following her Spiritual

Guide, crossed the ocean as an indentured servant
girl, soon after found herself imprisoned for debt, but
finally became a valiant evangelist, travelling extensively on both sides of the Atlantic, and in the
Barbadoes, as minister of a church which she was in
childhood taught to ridicule.

In the list of our martyrs are Catharine Evans and
Sarah Cheveer from whose lips the voice of Christian
hymns echoed within the walls of the Inquisition of
Malta, and who desired that the same "Good News,"
in the sweet language of song might be sent to the
ends of the earth, that all nations might "Praise the
Lord."

In the fields of Christian philanthropy the name of
Elizabeth Fry has long been held forth as a model of
devotion and self sacrifice, not only within the Friends'
Society alone, but in the Christian world at large.

To attempt to present the biography of one who
filled a very different sphere of Christian usefulness
and Gospel service, might seem a difficult task,
were it not that intimate acquaintance and close
spiritual fellowship has made it a comparatively easy
effort to the writer.

I may observe however that the sphere of woman's
influence and labor in the land of the Montezumas
has ever been very different from that of her sisters
in England and America, but few have left any record, and most of these few records are the poetic
effusions of gentle minds, full of tenderness and
pathos, the distinguishing traits of the Spanish
female.

Perhaps my readers will pardon a still further
digression, and allow me to cite one of those memorable examples that stand out in bold relief in the
annals of Mexican history, and it will show the
obstacles which woman had to struggle against
during the three centuries of Spanish rule in New
Spain, as Mexico was then called.

In the midst of the Spanish colonial domination during the seventeenth century, in the midst of blind superstition and bigotry, in a society ruled by these preoccupying influences a bright star shone forth, known in the cloister and in literary circles as Sister Juana Inés de la Cruz. Her true name was Juana Inés de Asbaje y Cantillana, i. e. her father's surname was Asbaje and her mother's maiden name was Cantillana, she was born in the village of San Miguel Nepantla, among the corrugated folds of the volcano of Popocatapetl.

When only three years of age she followed an older sister to a kind of school known as "The Friends," (which was not a Quaker institution by any means,) and there she soon learned to read. Then she heard of a University in Mexico where the sciences were taught, i. e. to young men, and she continually pleaded with her mother to change her clothing, dress her as a boy and send her to the University. Her mother had no inclination to favor female suffrage, and denied the repeated petitions of her daughter.

Notwithstanding this refusal, little Juana took to learning like a duck to the water, and as they said that some kinds of food were unfavorable to progress in study, she refrained her appetite and refused to partake of them. This was especially the case with cheese, of which she was naturally fond, and to what extent it may tend to rudeness and hinder education we leave our readers to judge from experience.

Her biographer supposes that the sight of that colossal mountain, and the awe inspiring scenery which surrounded her, had an influence in preparing her mind for that poetic susceptibility which has immortalized her name.

Such was her progress, and such the fame which was noised abroad, that when only seven years of age she was presented in the court of the Viceroy

Juana Inés de la Cruz.

and examined by the wise men of the country to find whether her learning was innate or acquired.

She was slender, and her dark eyes and silken tresses gave her such a beautiful appearance that the natives of those warm regions compared her, as they do the Virgin Mary, to a feathery palm waving in the gentle breeze of summer.

The Marquis of Mancera was at that time Viceroy of New Spain, and in speaking of this wonderful examination he says: "As a royal war ship would defend itself from a few canoes which attacked it, thus did Juana Inés resolve the questions, arguments and replies that one by one were propounded to her by that illustrious company."

It seemed impossible for her to go forward with her studies without embracing the monastic life, and the counsels of Antonio Nuñez, a famous Jesuit priest induced her to adopt that course.

It was no small sacrifice for her to exchange the splendid society of the viceroyal court for the solitude of the monastery. Whilst fulfilling the routine of nunnery restrictions, and exercising charity toward the poor and the sick, she devoted a considerable portion of her time to the study of such books as were accessible, and thus passed the earlier years of her *religious imprisonment.*

But the preoccupations of that dark period, the susceptibility of the theologians and confessors, at last reached in her asylum the girl, that in the narrow bounds of a Mexican cloister, was eclipsing the brightest literary stars that arrived from Spain.

You must not, dear reader, suppose that Mexico was devoid of literary minds in that epoch. A printing press had been busily at work for a century in the capital, and among other valuable works the great "Vocabulary of the Spanish and Mexican languages," had already been issued, long ere any press had reached the English provinces.

There was however in Mexico, as in Spain at that time, a saying that when any one was becoming learned; "he was in danger of becoming a Lutheran," that is, a Protestant. Such were the fears that were entertained about Juana Inés de la Cruz, and the books were taken away from her, and but limited opportunity was given to her to employ her pen, which however she did to some extent in controversial letters to celebrated divines. But in the midst of this privation Juana was taken seriously ill, and the physicians, who seem to have had some insight into her difficulties, prescribed reading and study as essential to her existence. A celebrated sermon of Father Vicyra had been published, and caused great notoriety, when Juana wrote a refutation of it, which was answered by another document from the Bishop of Puebla, who considered "the erudition of Juana as very improper for her sex." Her answer to the Bishop is one of the most noteworthy documents which that century can furnish us, written though it was by the creole girl of San Miguel Nepantla. She defends female education with rare energy for a woman of that period, and boldly says: "How without logic should I understand the general and special rules of composition? How without rhetoric should I understand the rules, discourses and figures of speech? How without natural history should I understand the nature of animals and the symbols of the ancient sacrifices? How without arithmetic should I be able to compute the years, days, months and hours of the mysterious hebdomads of Daniel, and others which require a knowledge of the nature, concordance and properties of numbers? How without a knowledge of the rules and parts which constitute History, should I understand the descriptions of sieges in the Historical Books? And how without a legal knowledge shall I be able to understand the Books of the Law of Moses?" After this noble *résumé* of the needs of female education, she like every protesting writer, quotes largely from the Gospels and Early Fathers of the Church in defense of woman's position in the world and in the church.

The books were again denied her by the *Superiora* or Preceptress of the nunnery, and then she studied the nature or character of her companions, watched the plays of the children and made geometrical investigations on the lines described by a top which the children kept whirling on the parallel lines of the roof of her cell; observing in the silence of the night, and the deeper silence of the monastery, the march of the stars, the changes of morning and evening twilight, and studying the laws of perspective in the movement of visible objects.

The portrait which adorns this narrative was copied from one painted by her own hand, the original being a most admirable painting.

In the midst of her trials from the privation of books, a terrible epidemic made its appearance in the Convent of San Geronimo, only one in ten of those attacked surviving its devastating influence, and after taking assiduous care of her sister nuns, she was taken with the disease and died on the 17th of April 1695. She has been styled for her talent the "Tenth Muse," and the "American Phœnix," and not only in Mexico but in South America her poems have excited universal admiration.

It might be proper here to remark that during the colonial administration the mail facilities between the various Spanish provinces of Central and South America were nearly equal to those of our own country a century later, and a unity of language and identity of interest bound the provinces of that time as strongly together as the independent republics are now united and the interchange of thought aided, by the facilities of the Postal Union.

Education was not then general, nor is it now, but there were then many noble minds aspiring to emancipate themselves from the thrall of intolerance and superstition, and since the independence of these governments became fully established these minds have multiplied, the press has everywhere become a moving power and the interchange of thought has been continually binding Latin Americans, as they prefer to be called, more and more closely in the bonds of intelligent brotherhood, and these minds thus brought into unison are leavening the masses. The new mold will vary according to the elevating influences brought to bear upon it.

Ere leaving the subject of woman's position in Mexico I must not forget that in a widely different and less womanly field, in the sphere of political movements and military achievements, aside from Doña Marina the guide and spy of Cortez, two names are indelibly written on the pages of Mexican history. When a few enthusiastic minds began thinking about the independence of Mexico, they gathered in the parlor of the *Corregidor* of the city of Querétaro to discuss so momentous a question. This group consisted of Miguel Hidalgo y Castillo, priest of Dolores, Colonels Aldama and Allende, and the *Corregidor* and his strong-minded wife. The men seemed fearful of so daring a movement. Allende with tropical ardor urged a trial of the plan, Hidalgo assured them that the initiators of such a movement rarely lived to see their ideas achieved, and this reasoning had well nigh discouraged the group when Josefa Ortiz de Dominguez analyzed their plans and assured them of their ultimate triumph. The plot was discovered and among the first to suffer imprisonment were the *Corregidor* and his wife, who suffered long years of imprisonment ere the uprising of Iturbide in Iguala achieved the independence of Mexico and the *Corregidora* was hailed as a heroine of the independence.

Another name to be mentioned in this connection is that of Maria Antonia de la Serna, wife of Felipe de la Garza, known for her daring enterprises as *la Generala*. She was left a widow early in life, with a nephew, adopted as a son, and with an ample fortune at her disposal. She settled at Soto la Marina, then a very small settlement, and was united in marriage to the commanding officer of that port; which was incorporated as a village at her suggestion, and the beautiful catholic church with its sweet-toned bells was a gift of her munificence to the village. She once fitted out a steamer to bring military supplies to her adopted son, Jesus de la Serna, in his struggle to become governor of Tamaulipas; and was doubtless the counsellor of her husband in the arrest of Iturbide, an act his fidelity to his government required at his hand, although in all the movement he showed the highest personal appreciation of his imperial prisoner and did all in his power to avert from him the terrible fate to which a decree of Congress had condemned the ex-emperor.

Leaving then the sphere of poetic genius and military prowess we will look at an humbler but worthier figure in Mexican social life.

ANCIENT AZTEC WARRIORS IN FULL DRESS.

A HOME IN "TIERRA CALIENTE."

# CHAPTER II.

BIRTHPLACE OF ANGELA AGUILAR, WITH A GENERAL
SKETCH OF THE COAST REGION OF TAMAULIPAS, AND
THE ORIGIN AND CHARACTER OF ITS INHABITANTS.

ERHAPS few things could be more widely different than the scenery and personage of the preceding chapter and those we now introduce to the
attention of the reader. He must therefore be
prepared to come down in imagination from the lofty
heights of Popocatepetl to the flat sandy shores of
Tamaulipas, from the pure air and undulating scenery
of the *Tierra Templada* to the dense forest shades and
malarial atmosphere which gird the banks of Rio de
la Marina, in *Tierra Caliente;* from the wondrous
poetical genius of a pure descendant of Castile, to
the unassuming manners of a dark-eyed daughter
of the mixed race, who but for the strange dispensa-
tions of Providence would have lived and died a
peasant girl or at most the wife of some poor farmer
or stock raiser in the wilds of Tamaulipas. I must
however take into consideration that the reader has
not like the writer, passed a decade in this Mexican
State, whose scenes however rough and homely have
become as familiar to him as the pastures of the old
homestead. 11

Please place a map before you and you will find near the Gulf of Mexico, and about midway between Matamoros and Tampico, the village of Soto la Marina. You may at first suppose that it is situated at the mouth of a river bearing very nearly the same name. Soto la Marina *(The Marine Forest,)* is situated about thirty miles from the mouth of the river, whose banks are lined with magnificent forests of giant tropical trees. The forests still abound in jaguars and other tropical animals and countless flocks of parrots, whilst the water is prolific in alligators and the manatee, or aquatic cow. The hunt of this latter animal is very interesting and its capture a day of rejoicing for the whole community, who with notable neighborly kindness give freely what they have freely received.

This port was entered at a very early date by the Spanish coasting vessels, and as they rarely drew more than three or four feet of water they found no difficulty in crossing the bar and ascending the river as far as the present site of the village, which was founded about the year 1750 under the direction of Colonel José de Escandon, the colonizer and pacifier of Tamaulipas.

He marched through the country with trains of emigrants, leaving a definite number in each eligible site for a village, supplying their necessities, leaving them under the political care of a captain, and each of these settlements was furnished with a Catholic priest, who aside from the spiritual care of the emigrants was expected to form a mission a little way from the village and if possible *domesticate* the Indians.

The native races to the southward of Rio de la Marina seem to have been powerful at the time of the conquest, as Cortez was defeated at the pass of Chile near the present site of Tampico of Tamaulipas by 60,000 warriors organized in this section as early as 1521. A little later however the conquest was

effected and the only record of the ancient greatness
of the natives consists of the ruins of ten cities,
buried by the rank vegetation, and lying on both sides
of the Tamesí river, and whose capital was probably
the city whose ruins are in Sierra de la Palma, a low
chain of mountains about twenty seven miles west of
Altamira, a village on the shores of Lake Champayan.

Whatever may have been the violence exercised by
the conquerors, and the bloody scenes which marked
the conquest, we may be permitted to state that some
of the viceroys were friendly to the native races, and
did all in their power to settle them peacefully in
villages and encourage them in the arts of civilization.

The idea of enslaving the native race was brought
by the conquerors from Cuba, and perhaps no man
at that time was more conscientious upon that subject than Cortez, whose will plainly shows his misgivings upon that point. Bartholomew las Casas,
bishop of Chiapas, wrote energetically upon this
subject as early as 1540, and he by no means stood
alone.

"With respect to the slaves, natives of New Spain, alike those
taken in war and those held for redemption, as there are many
doubts and opinions as to whether these can be conscientiously so held,
and up to the present it has not been determined; I command my son
and successor Martin, and those who follow him in my estate, that they
use all diligence to investigate the matter, and do whatever may be
most convenient for the full discharge of my conscience and their own."

WILL OF CORTEZ. ARTICLE 39.

"I also command that as aside from the tributes which I have
received from my vassals aforesaid, I have received from them other
personal and real services, and as there are diverse opinions as to
whether these services can be conscientiously received, I order that due
diligence be used to ascertain what services I may have received more
than pertained to me, and that pay and restitution be made wherever
it appears justly due."—IDEM. ARTICLE 41.

Luis de Velasco II. nearly a century before Penn
made his treaty with the Indians under the elm at

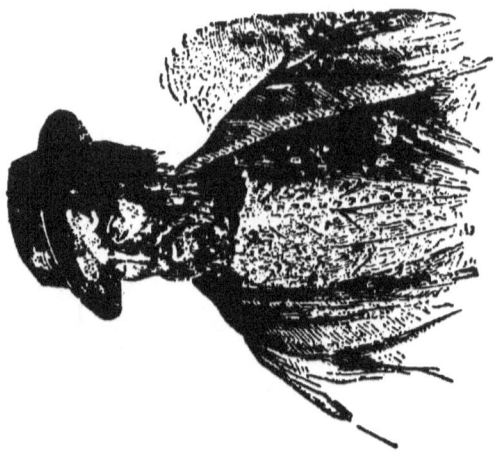

**Hernan Cortez.**

Conqueror of New Spain, Marquis of
the Valloy of Oaxaca, and Founder of the
Convent of Sta. Catarina in Culhuacan.

**Pedro de Alvarado.**

Conqueror of New Spain, called by the
Aztecs "Tonituah," Child of the Sun. Tried
in 1529 for his cruelty to the Aborigines.

Shackamaxon had made a treaty recompensing the undomesticated tribes of Central Mexico for the occupation of their territory by colonies of Tlaxcalans, who planted in their midst the elements of civilization, and although he was not able to entirely obliterate the servitude of the natives, their tasks were fixed by law as was also the salary they were to receive, and it was forbidden to employ them in the mines, or in any other notably severe and perilous occupation. The provinces of Zacatecas and San Luis Potosí were settled peacefully by this wise policy, which almost a century later the viceroy, Count Revilla-Gigedo endeavored to carry out in settling the province of Santander, now known as the Mexican State of Tamaulipas.

Perhaps he could not have found a person better fitted for this task than José de Escandon. Everywhere he manifested uniform kindness to the natives and these in return became his allies. Not far from the present site of Soto la Marina a large force of Indians approached his camp, and stationing a rearguard advanced to meet him, carrying a large supply of beans, sweet potatoes and pumpkins, which they presented him, receiving in return shawls and blankets. Their chief then asked for a gourd of water, and washed the hands of Escandon and such of his companions as he supposed to be chiefs, and then taking from his own body the *sayal* or native blanket, he wiped their hands, giving them to understand that this ceremony was emblematic of peace, friendship and alliance.

This friendship was interrupted a few days later because some natives, perhaps not knowing the value of horses, killed some of them with their arrows, one of them being killed in the pursuit which followed. This was however the only conflict which Escandon had with the natives whilst planting the villages of the whole central portion of Tamaulipas. His colonists had received one hundred dollars in silver for each family, supplies for the journey, and seeds for planting, as well as tools for farm work, and peacefully began to build their cabins in the forest.

The village of Soto la Marina was founded by 66 families, having a total force of 11 soldiers for their defence, making in all 289 settlers. This gives us an opportunity to see how far they considered themselves exempt from peril under the wise plans devised for them by the viceroy, Count Revilla-Gigedo, and carried out by Escandon, Lieutenant Captain General of the province.

The natives were of peaceful disposition and Escandon, judging from the general tenor of Mexican colonies, supposed that they would gradually gather to the settlements and become his dutiful subjects. In this he was not disappointed, but one of his fond hopes met with a reverse. He had expected to find the water on the bar at the mouth of Rio de la Marina of sufficient depth for ocean trade. His schooner *"Conquistadora"* had entered the harbor, but a minute examination made by his chief engineer Tienda de Cuervo demonstrated, on the one hand the shallowness of water, and on the other, the absence of any prominent landmarks by which vessels could recognize the entrance.

It is true that nearly a century earlier the caravels which crossed the ocean could have entered the river, as they only drew from three to five feet of water, but now only coasting vessels could be expected to engage in commerce with the newly established port. It is also probable that Tienda de Cuervo was influenced by the merchants of Vera Cruz to hinder its being opened to foreign trade.

The rapid increase in the tonnage of vessels coming from Cuba and Spain soon made it impracticable to use Soto la Marina as a port for foreign commerce, and thus it lost a great part of its importance.

It has however twice been the scene of great political movements of historic interest.

On the 15th of April 1817 an expedition of adventurers from England and the United States, with some fugitives from Mexico who favored the party which was struggling for independence, landed at Soto la Marina under the command of Francisco Javier Mina, who had headed the revolution of Navarre, to aid the insurgents.

The cause they came to defend had however been almost completely crushed before they arrived, and after repeated defeats Mina, like most other unfortunate revolutionists in Spanish America was taken prisoner and sentenced to be shot.

After the independence was achieved under the direction of Agustin de Iturbide, and the restless band who had hoped for a Republic instead of an Empire had obliged him to abdicate, following the track of Mina, he landed at Soto la Marina on the 14th of July 1824, and was immediately informed that a decree of Congress condemned him to death so soon as he landed in the country. Yet such was the confidence which the military commander of the town, Felipe de la Garza, had in Iturbide, that he placed the troops which were to conduct him to Padilla, capital of the state, under his command, hoping that the state legislature, or congress as it is called would in some way try to reprieve him, as he had brought no forces with him. His sentence was however confirmed and five days after landing at Soto la Marina, he was shot publicly in the plaza of Padilla, and his remains were buried under the ruins of the village chapel, from whence like those of Napoleon I. they were marched under triumphal arches to the city of Mexico and honorably placed among those of the heroes of independence.

Such is the mutability of human greatness and so slight the difference which history places between

a *patriot* and a *traitor*, that Mexican historians have
scarcely been able to to find to which class Iturbide
belongs.

Aside from these two disturbances the village of
Soto la Marina seems to have kept the even tenor
of its way, with no very great abundance of trade
and with but little importance in its agriculture, perhaps the trade in fish caught and salted at Pescade-
ria at the mouth of the river was the special thing
which drew traders from the interior to this port.

ITZA PICTURE WRITINGS.
SYMBOLIC AND IDEOGRAPHIC.

MOTECUHZOMA II. AND THE COMET OF CHAS. V.
FROM THE AZTEC PICTURE WRITINGS, DURAN'S CODEX.

# CHAPTER III.

BIRTH AND EARLY LIFE OF ANGELA AGUILAR Y ZÚÑIGA,
WITH AN INSIGHT INTO THE DOMESTIC LIFE OF THE
MEXICANS.

S we said in the preceding chapter, when these
villages were founded, a mission was established
near each of them, and in many cases on the
opposite bank of the stream upon which both
must rely for a supply of water. Gradually the natives began to serve the settlers, either in the culti-
vation of the small patches of corn and sugar-cane
or in the manual duties of the household, they became the hewers of wood and drawers of water, receiving in return a nominal salary, which was
usually paid in eatables and in the very scanty clothing which the laborers required. The laboring
men used only trowsers and a broad brimmed hat of
palm leaf when at work, yet they usually tried to
have a better holiday suit. In some villages the settlers became very wealthy and there was a notable
difference between the *hacendado* or proprietor and
the *peon* or laborer. This latter class found themselves bound to a perpetual servitude, as the wages

19

of a day laborer were only 25 cents and often less, and when extra expense was incurred, as for example when money was borrowed to pay the priest's fee for marriage, or the doctor's fee for services, they were hardly ever able, even during years of toil to emancipate themselves from the service of their employer. Their salary was paid by credit on the books and often a father died leaving a debt of $100 to $200 for his children to cancel by servitude.

There was however quite a numerous class of the poorer descendants of the settlers, and intermarriages between these and the natives became frequent until the process of amalgamation became quite general.

Indeed the settlers who came from the interior had already an admixture of Aztec and Tlascalan blood in their veins, for many of those families stood high in social life. When these mixed people testified in the courts the judge was obliged to record whether they were whites or Indians, and in doubtful cases would say, "*Se tiene por blanco,*" i. e. "He considers himself a white man."

At Soto la Marina both settlers and natives had to struggle with hard times and thus, except a few very wealthy families, the distinctions of caste began to fade away.

The change of laws in 1857 under the Liberal Government made provisions to emancipate the laboring class from perpetual servitude, only allowing one month of advance wages to be paid to a servant except at the risk of his employer. This law in many places is a dead letter, carefully concealed from the working class, and practically ignored by crafty judges.

As in most other Mexican villages along the coast, there are three distinct kinds of houses in general use in Soto la Marina, the wealthier class having stone houses with flat roofs made of heavy planking covered with *tejas,* formerly written *texas,* a kind of flat tile brick about seven inches square and one inch thick, three courses of which are laid on an inclined floor like roof, in a strong cement, which when dry becomes impervious to water. These flat roofs, as we may call them, are surrounded on three sides by a strong wall, making as they complete the buildings on all sides of a block a regular fortress, the yards being in the open court back of the houses, forming a general rendezvous in most cases for all the inhabitants of the block. Some of these inner yards have beautiful flowers, orange trees and other choice plants, which are hid entirely from the passer by, as the houses are built on a line with the sidewalk, with doors opening to the street. The second class of houses have the walls made of adobes, or sun dried bricks, which are much larger than our bricks, and the roofs are made of poles lashed together with thongs, or the strong fibre of the maguey or century plant, and thatched with palm leaves, or swamp grass. The dry flower-stalks of the century plant are used for rafters wherever the plant abounds, especially at the neighoring village of Jimenez.

The third class have the same kind of roof, but the walls instead of being of adobes are made of cross poles tied to upright forks, when small bundles of reeds are tied in an upright position to the cross-poling, and the whole is plastered outside and inside with strong adobe mortar. This mortar is prepared by making a firm mud from a strong clayey earth, and mixing in dried grass chopped about two inches in length, supplying the place of hair in our plastering. The stone buildings have a floor of hard cement, the adobe houses sometimes have them of brick but most of these, like the third class, known as *guano* houses have only the earth for a floor.

In one of the houses of the first class lived a family by the name of Zúñiga, who were owners of the house and lot, but had little else of earthly goods.

In this humble home the mother died when giving birth to a daughter, which was at once placed in charge of her god-mother, Maria Antonia de la Serna, by whom, with other orphan children she was reared, yet she retained her proper name Francisca Zúñiga.

As her foster daughters grew up she had no small trouble to prevent their receiving visits from the young men of the village, and thus it was with great secrecy and slyness that they were able to send letters and receive replies from their sweet hearts. Several times the mother surprised her daughter Francisca at the little gate of their yard, opening to the street, talking with a young man whose large black eyes had an almost fascinating power over those with whom he associated. Very naturally mamma did not like to see them talking thus slyly and gave her daughter a sound thrashing, and tried to let the young pretender understand that his absence was more welcome than his presence.

The young man was a day laborer, with no earthly goods, and more than that, he was a widower with a little daughter to care for. The mother was inflexible, the daughter equally so, and the young man was determined to gain if possible and it seemed as though the judge would have to be called on to set aside the maternal authority, as under certain circumstances they are empowered to do, but finally the opposition gave way and the marriage was effected. For a little while young Aguilar and his wife lived in one room of the stone building which had been her home, but a *guano* house with a palm leaf roof was soon ready and thither the young couple removed. In this humble structure their first daughter was born August 2d 1858, and when she was but a few weeks old her pious parents took her to the parish church where she was baptized as Angela and as she had a right to both paternal and maternal surnames, her true name was Angela Aguilar y Zúñiga. But as we are to know that she was a pet, her pet name takes the diminutive *ita* and we shall for some years. call her Angelita.

Although she was the pet, the poverty of her father scarcely ever allowed them any spare change for buying oranges or candy, and the neighbor who chanced to give her either was looked upon as a real benefactor, both by her and by her doting parents.

Judging from analogy we may suppose that after being emancipated from the swaddling clothes of infancy, except a holiday attire, which was usually kept carefully laid away, she was not much encumbered with clothing during the week, yet on the Sabbath morning she was clothed ready to go to the church, dip her tiny hand in the font of holy water and make the sign of the cross on her forehead.

She was also taught two prayers to the Virgin Mary and the Lord's Prayer, which she was taught to repeat thus, the Lord's Prayer once and the prayers to the Virgin each five times, and when she went to the parish church the whole service was a repetition of the same prayers, in the same relative proportion, the priest leading, and the worshippers, who were all kneeling on the floor, following in a low voice the continual recital of the same prayers. A few pictures of the Saints were purchased, and sprinkled with holy water by the priest for the small sum of twenty five cents each, and one corner of their humble cabin was arranged so as to form a kind of altar before which they could kneel to count beads and say prayers. Some small printed prayers or amulets were also purchased from the priest, as preventatives of certain diseases as well as remedies for many of the evils flesh is heir to. This was all the more necessary as there was no regular drug store in the village and patent medicines had not begun to compete with prayers and amulets in public favor.

Otherwise we have few particulars about the early life of Angelita. We can however very readily imagine how she played with the other little girls of the village, how they would go down to the river and bathe in the flowing stream, and then sit on the bank to admire the bright green parrots with their golden heads and bright red epaulets on their -wings, . and listen to their terrific clamor. It may often have been her lot to watch the little patch of corn her father was cultivating and scare the parrots away as children do the crows in more northern latitudes.

MEXICAN RANCH LIFE.
WOMAN CARRYING WATER.

Her parents were all the time struggling with poverty, and it was finally decided that as labor was so very scarce they must move out to some ranch where labor was better requited and the cost of living would be less. They accordingly carried out this plan. It was in some respects quite a disagreeable change to Angelita. She had to leave her old playmates and the gayer life of the village, for the more isolated life of the Mexican ranch. Quite a change now took place in her outward appearance, she wore a long dress, reaching to her ankles, and when sitting carefully threw it over her feet, and was soon taught to laugh about the short dresses and pantelets of the village girls, who were so earnest about having shoes on their feet when walking on the street, or going to the chapel. There was an abundance of milk, and plenty of cheese, and as she had no educational opportunities she was not taught to abstain from the latter.

Here as in the village however the forty days of Lent must be carefully observed, and during this time they must eat plenty of greens, especially the tender shoots of the prickly pear, *(cactus,)* and limit their meat to fish only.

These was an abundance of wild honey, known as the *panal* or comb, found in nests on the limbs of the trees much like the nests of our wasps. She was taught sedulously to avoid the tarantulas, a very large and venomous spider, the scorpions and rattlesnakes, and very frequently suffered severely from the stings of the red ants, which are as painful as those of the scorpion. Our readers may not be aware that the ant is very nearly allied to the bee, that some ants make honey, and that being very aromatic, some varieties of the ant are dried and pounded into a paste which is sold as a sweet meat in most parts of South America, though not *known* in this part of Mexico. By simply tasting an ant you will become assured of their virtues as edible food, and we learn that the children of Americans living in South America are excessively fond of ant paste.

However we must not let our readers suppose that such was the food of Angelita. Her principal food, like that of the poorer class in Mexico consisted simply of *tortillas* and *frijoles*, or slap-jacks and beans. Corn for making *tortillas* is first boiled in lime-water, so that the hull can readily be removed, it is then ground on an inclined stone with a square hand piece, tapering toward either end, each of the four sides of which are of a different fineness. Whilst the process of grinding progresses water is occasionally thrown on and the corn instead of being ground into meal is at once reduced to dough of the right consistency which is slapped out into thin cakes and hastily cooked on a thin piece of iron or pottery ware, usually set on some thin pieces of brick, so as to leave room for the coals underneath.

The bean soup is usually served in a saucer, a folded piece of *tortilla* serving as a spoon, which so soon as it becomes moistened is swallowed and another spoon manufactured. Butter is not extensively made so that when any sauce is used on the tortillas it is made of red pepper pods fried in lard, the very best being made of red and cayenne pepper pods fried in lard and seasoned with onions and Dutch cheese, made from sour milk.

In the villages knives, forks and spoons are quite generally used by the well-to-do residents. Ranch people occasionally kill beef cattle; and deer, antelopes, rabbits, hares and other wild game are very abundant, the wild hog and the armadillo being considered as delicacies.

MEXICAN ORANGE GIRL.

# CHAPTER IV.

Early religious training. Death of her father,
Removal to San Fernando, where the history
of Father Lozano the first Mexican reformer
is introduced and his teachings reviewed.

THEIR residence in the hacienda was of several years duration, but was terminated by a sad bereavement; the death of her father. Her mother found herself obliged to take full charge of the two daughters, and three months after the death of her husband, gave birth to a son. She could not well find work on the farm, and the experience of her friends induced her to try to get a place as house-servant in a village. She accordingly removed to the village of San Fernando, which stands on a bluff, on the bank of Rio de Conchas, ordinarily a small stream, but in the wet season becoming very formidable. It was not difficult for Angelita, who was now quite a girl, to accommodate herself to village life, and as she could attend the services of the parish church, her former religious earnestness was renewed, and she became well known for her devotional nature, the pet of the pious women of the village from whon she received many kindnesses.

Her mother was house servant for a widower, who had a child to care for, and although he did not hinder their attending the services, he did not parti-

27

cipate in their religious zeal. He had been for several years in care of his uncle, who was for some time
priest of the village, and under whose direction the
parish church was built, as an inscribed tablet in-
forms the passer by. A like tablet over the entrance
to the cemetery tells us that its beautiful ornamented
wall was also one of the improvements carried out
during the curacy of Father Lozano. The promulga-
tion of the Reform Laws of 1857 had awakened the
naturally earnest mind of this priest and as he inher-
ited a large library of theological books from a relative who was a priest, he began studying the New
Testament, following the Catholic version of Father
Scio, in order to see whether a *Liberal* could be a
Christian. The reader must understand that the Catholic Bishops were denouncing the *Liberal Government* as an ungodly institution, and fulminating
their anathemas against its leaders. When the father
of the aforementioned widower died in Victoria, capital of the State, it being known that he was a *Liberal* the Bishop refused to allow the church bell to
be rung for his burial, or even admit the corpse inside the church edifice. Thus Father Lozano began
studying to see whether his relatives who served the
*Liberal Government* must be refused like favors at
his hand. He found to his surprise that the teachings of Jesus Christ and his Apostles as recorded
in the New Testament were as different from those
taught by the Romish Church as light is from darkness. As he continued reading it seemed as though
he found prophecies of and warnings against those
very doctrines and practices which were the distinguishing features of his church, and those very protests of the *Liberal Party* seemed to be the echoes of
the early teachers of Christianity against spiritual
wickedness in high places. There were special reasons why the question of the celibacy of the clergy
should occupy his attention, because their irregular

conduct and the abuse made of the confessional for the seduction of young girls, which had awakened energetic protests from the Liberals, were creating great sensation. He had read the new law opening the way for priests to legitimize their children, usually known as their *nephews* and *nieces*, and as he was desirous of doing so himself, he made a special study of this matter.

As he was reading I. Tim. 4: 3, he saw that "Forbidding to marry, and commanding to abstain from meats," was a sure test whereby he might know the apostate church, from the true church. The illusions of a life-time vanished in a moment. His long fastings had been utterly unavailing. God was looking for a clean heart and not an empty stomach. As he read the qualifications of a Bishop, and found that "to be husband of one wife" and to "have his family in subjection," were desirable evidences of fitness for the station, whilst he had supposed celibacy an indispensable requisite, he was still more inclined to fear that he was a minister of the church of Antichrist. It seemed to him that a Liberal could be a New Testament Christian and that a reformation of the Church was necessary; for he had reason to believe that others like himself were seeking to know the true basis of Christianity, and would accept the testimony of the Holy Scriptures, so soon as they heard its teachings. The early steps of his alienation from Romanism had been noted by the other priests and had led to his removal to the curacy of Santa Barbara, a very unhealthy location and where his enemies hoped that disease might cut short his existence. However his health improved considerably by the change, whilst his wealth enabled him to furnish the poor people with rice and other grains for sowing their crops, charging a lighter rate of premium when the crop was gathered than the wealthy residents were accustomed to do. His philantropy

soon gained the hearts of his parishioners and they
were ready to listen to his counsels and looked up
to him with more than the usual reverence which
they felt toward their "*Father*," as you may remember
ber that Roman Catholics call their priests, although
it be expressly forbidden in the New Testament.

He soon after made an application to the State
Congress in order to legitimize his children, and
although proceeding according to the provision of the
law, he was cast into prison by order of Governor
Serna, where he was kept for several months. The
next session of congress was held by new delegates
and after a very animated discussion his petition was
granted, and he obtained his liberty.

He was well aware that this step would bring
upon him the censures of the Bishop and perhaps
excommunication, and he at once prepared for the
struggle by spending some months in his largest hacienda,
cienda, occupied closely with the New Testament, and
in preparing a brief *résumé* of its teachings, which
he published under the title of "El Sacerdote Evangé-
lico," or "The Evangelical Priest." This book was
publicly ratified by his congregation, so that the
Bishop found that he had not to deal with a single
heretic, but with a seceding congregation. When his
envoys came to read the excommunication from the
pulpit, they found the door closed, and the whole
town so excited that they could only fulfil their mission by pasting the excommunication on the doors
of the church from whence it was soon torn
down by the indignant residents. So great was the
the excitement that the Mayor fearing that some
danger might await the envoys, took them into
custody and sent them to Tampico as disturbers of
the public peace. It is probable that blood would
have been shed had not Father Lozano addressed the
people explaining to them the peaceable nature of the
Gospel, and that as the Kingdom of Christ is not of

this world, therefore his servants are not to advance it by carnal weapons.

There are several points in which Father Lozano held views very similar to those of the Society of Friends, for aside from his peace principles he was opposed to oaths which had recently been forbidden in courts of law by the Liberal Government.

He says; "We hold that the oath has been justly omitted in the formulas of the Mexican Government, and is discarded by the Mexican Church, in accordance with the Apostolic doctrines."

The humility of his closing words, in bold contrast with the dogmatism of most Reformers, merits our attention. "My doctrines, fallible because they are set forth by a man of limited capacity, admit as many reforms and observations as may be made upon them with the Gospels and Nature before you, for these are the only books which express the certain will of God, and the positive truth of all things, where man must seek them if he aspire to know them. Whilst these observations are being examined, I would again ask the indulgence of my readers, and incite the venerable Mexican clergy to cast aside all preoccupation and partiality and retracing their steps, cease to be the executioners of their fold, and embracing first the Reform, incline the people to do the same, as it is the only thing which can save the dignity and liberty of mankind, and can alone make them a truly Christian clergy, the only principles to which are promised the peace and civilization of the world, which God has entrusted to the probity, integrity, intelligence and fidelity of his ministers, when he commanded them to preach his evangelical doctrines of reconciliation, peace and universal love."

TYPES OF MEXICAN COSTUMES IN THE INTERIOR.

GOING TO MARKET.    INDIANS IN HOLIDAY DRESS.    CREOLES.

# CHAPTER V.

NOTWITHSTANDING the favorable circumstances which had led B.... S.... to imbibe Protestant principles; he does not seem to have in any way tried to instil them into the minds of the widow and three little ones now placed by so singular a providence under his roof.

Francisca Zúñiga appears to have occupied herself almost exclusively in the domestic cares of the household of B.... S.... and had but little time to care for her own children, but had the pleasure of their company. Angelita was now a robust girl of about a dozen summers, and spent the week days in the village free School. By the way Mexico has a system of Free Schools, and compulsory education is enforced in most of the cities. The elementary branches and embroidery of various kinds are taught, also worsted figure work on perforated paper. A text book on "Urbanity" or "Good Manners" is considered indispensable and forms the basis of that courtesy and politeness so noticeable in Mexican society.

The Lancasterian system is generally used, the teachers appointing a monitor for each class, who listens with a cautious ear to the loud study of his pupils, for all study quite loudly; and several long benches arranged around the sides of the room pre-

33                                                    D

sent a decided analogy with several Sabbath School classes in active recitation in a small chapel in our own country. A foreigner would at once suppose that the noise would make study impossible. This is not the case however, for they become so accustomed to it that the monitor will readily note an error in pronunciation by any one of his class and at once recognizes the voice of the one who made the mistake and calls him to order, just as readily as a weaving girl in our factories recognizes which one of her looms has a broken thread and stops it in order to repair it.

Silent study has been introduced in some places, but by far the most general method is as above described. Our little Angelita made fair progress in the elementary branches, but the brevity of their residence in that village and want of educational facilities in the ranch where she had spent her childhood prevented her acquiring more than the elementary branches.

The widow of the owner of the ranch where they had lived before coming to San Fernando appears to have moved to the village soon after they did and she became the *madrina* or spiritual mother of Angelita, and being a very devoted Catholic took her little charge to Mass every Sabbath morning. The recollections of the religious exercises she had been accustomed to see in Soto la Marina were now revived. Besides this San Fernando was a more aristocratic village, with a very strong predominance of pure Spanish blood, and much more *religious*, if we may give this name to such superstitious Romanism as was there in vogue. Aside from the name of "Presbyter Ramon Lozano" on the front of the Catholic Church and over the gateway of the cemetery, nothing of his doctrines seems to have remained in the place. Thus Angelita, became a zealous Catholic, was always to be seen at Mass, repeating the prescribed number of prayers to the Virgin Mary with one Lord's Prayer for every ten of these.

Having been confirmed she must now begin to confess regularly to the village priest, and she carefully watched every thought and action so as to give an accurate account of every sin in thought, word or deed.

Besides the numerous fasts prescribed by the church she found it necessary to impose upon herself extra ones in order to have money to give her confessor every time she received absolution for past sins, thus she began that peculiar course of abnegation which won for her a distinguished place in the Catholic circles of San Fernando and Matamoros. You must bear in mind that she had not as yet listened to a sermon or exposition of Gospel Truth. In Mexico so far as we have been able to ascertain there is no preaching in the Catholic Churches except where Protestant churches have heen organized; nor are there any seats, but the whole audience, almost exclusively women, kneel on the floor and repeat in concert with the priest "Salves" and "Ave Marías" to the Virgen and either one Lord's Prayer after each five or after each ten prayers to the Most Holy Mary.

The favorite prayer in all Spanish American countries is the "Ave María" or "Hail Mary," and is as follows:—"Dios te Salve María llena eres de gracia, el Señor es contigo, bendita tú entre las mugeres, y bendito el Fruto de tu vientre Jesus. Santa Maria, Madre de Dios, ruega por nosotros pecadores, ahora y en la ahora de nuestra muerte, Amen Jesus." This may be literally translated thus:—God save thee Mary full of grace, the Lord is with thee, blessed art thou among women, and blessed is the Fruit of thy Womb Jesus. Holy Mary Mother of God, pray for us sinners, now and in the hour of our death Amen Jesus." I have carefully retained the punc-

tuation and capitals as used in their prayer books,
though not adopting either as grammatical.

The "Ave Maria" or "angelical salutation" came to
be used as an almost universal salutation when
speaking to any one who is so busily occupied as not
to notice you, or when trying to call at the door or
gateway of a ranch to ask for lodgings or inquire the
way.

The introduction of Protestant Chrsitianity gave
rise to an amusing incident. My reader will consider
that "Ave" means bird in Spanish and this gave
place to a little play on words.

Two men were travelling along when calling at a
ranch the Romanist called out as usual at the top of
his voice "Ave Maria," when the other answered
"Maria no fue gallina," "Mary was not a hen," i, e.
Mary was not a bird.

The Salve is a longer form of prayer to the Virgin
and is next in popularity to the Ave Maria.

Angelita soon had all these prayers so fixed in her
mind that she could repeat them hour after hour as
she knelt before some picture of the Virgin, and
great was her confidence in Mary as "Advocate of
sinners," the "True Mediator" and many similar
terms which Romanists apply to her, often neglect-
ing to bestow them upon Jesus Christ, not so much
from any intentional effort to rob him, as in letting
"Mary" so fill their minds that they do not see Jesus
clearly in his glorious mediatorial work, and manifold
attributes which pertain only to a Divine Being. The
exchange of mediators has been so entire that all
the great features of the life of Jesus have been
engrafted on her biography, from her "immaculate
conception" or being born without sin, to her glorious "assumption" or ascent to heaven, thus equal-
ling her to the Divinity and then bestowing upon
her the title of Mother of God and Queen of Heaven

by these means impressing the masses with a belief that she is equal with God.

There are special reasons why the Mexican people have come to look upon the Virgin as their "Advocate." The Aztecs found little difficulty in exchanging their great goddess Tonantzin for Mary of Nazareth so soon as she appeared as a lovely Indian maiden near the ancient altar of their goddess. However to avoid any show of unfairness I will give the Catholics a hearing. I copy from a Catholic paper, "La Voz de la Patria," of December 18th, 1881. "The 12th of December is the great feast of Mexico, when hope arises anew in the most tried souls. The beautiful day and sublime scenes of Tepeyecatl are brought to mind, the Queen of Heaven, talking lovingly of our nation's prosperity with a poor Indian, despised by the world, but whose fidelity and purity of soul commended him to God, because in the sight of God not the rich and powerful, but humility and purity attract the favor of Infinite Mercy, thus the Queen of Heaven, who could only see as God sees, passing by the rich and powerful deigned to speak to an humble Indian, making him rich promises for our good. She wished that a temple should be erected wherein to honor her, and in which she could show forth mercy to such as should invoke her blessing, and make known their petitions, and has left us painted on the blanket *(ayate)* of the happy Indian her precious image as Holy Mary of Guadalupe, in testimony of her partiality to us. Three hundred and fifty years have passed since these miracles took place, and the heavenly painting which the August Mother of the Redeemer, and beloved Mother of the Mexicans left with him as a memorial portrait, exists among us and is venerated in the magnificent temple which in fulfillment of their vow the piety of our fathers built to her memory, and copies of this beautiful picture are found in almost all our temples and in our homes. On this image are written, says a recent writer, in divine characters *the manifest destiny of Mexico*, against which vainly cavil those who without raising their eyes from the earth, consider themselves the supreme arbiters of the fate of countries, as though there were not over all their thoughts an infinitely wise and merciful providence on which our destiny depends. We doubt not, should she not lose it by her evil deeds, the manifest destiny of Mexico will be to receive without ceasing the distinguished benefits conferred by Divine Goodness and the special protection of the Mother of the Most High."

For over two hundred years the miraculous appearance of the Virgin of Guadalupe was celebrated as a national feast day and her historians quoted it as a historical fact. That the people should have adhered so firmly to imposture and have believed that the painting now in the temple at Guadalupe was painted by miracle, that they should have believed that the canvass on which it was painted was the *ayate* or blanket of Juan Diego, the poor Indian, would seem impossible, did we not reflect that fanaticism *is blind.* I will now briefly sum up the opinions of those who deny the miracle.

1 The *ayates* of the Aztecs were made of the fibres of the maguey or American aloe, like our coarse roping, whilst the painting is on a smooth mat made of palm leaves.

2 The prayer sanctioned by Pope Benedict XIV. In his brief he refused to say that it was *miraculously painted* and substituted that it was said to be *admirably painted.*

3 Neither the *mass* nor the *prayer* mention the miraculous appearance.

4 The catholic historian Sahagun says about it: "Near the Mounts there are three or four places where the Aztecs frequently offered solemn sacrifices,

to which people came from remote places. One of these is called Tepeyac, the Spaniards called it Tepeaquilla and now it is called *Our Lady of Guadalupe.* In this place they had the Mother of the gods, Tonantzin, which means *Our Mother.* There they offered many sacrifices, and people came from a distance of twenty leagues or more, strong men and women, young men and maidens, all said: let us go up to the feast of Tonantzin.

"And now that the church of *Our Lady of Guadalupe* has been built there, she is also called Tonantzin. From whence came the foundation of this Tonantzin we cannot ascertain, though the word signifies that ancient Tonantzin. This thing should be remedied because the name of the Mother of God is not Tonantzin but Diosinantzin. It appears to be a wile of Satan to palliate idolatry under the exchange of this name Tonantzin, and people come from as far to worship this new Tonantzin, and whilst there are many chapels of the Virgin they do not frequent them but come as before from far and near to the shrine of Tonantzin." The Viceroy Don Martin Enriquez and the chaplain of the hermitage of Guadalupe ignored the *aparicion milagrosa* and do not appear to have believed it even when the King asked that the Archbishop should visit it and take account of the collections and donations received there from people who flocked there for healing as they now do to the shrine of the Virgin of Lourdes in France. Superstition however makes people believe against all outward evidences.

ALTEC GOD TEOTL, THE SUN.

# CHAPTER VI.

A COLPORTEUR VISITS SAN FERNANDO. REMOVAL TO MATAMOROS, AND FIRST ACQUAINTANCE WITH PROTESTANTISM. ATTENDS OUR MEETING FOR THE FIRST TIME.

THE reader will pardon our presenting these horrid pictures of the actual state of the religion called Christianity in Mexico, prior to the advent of Protestant Christianity, with the open Bible, the most powerful of all forces to tear down the firm walls of superstition and bigotry. Such was the religion that Angela Aguilar had been taught to revere and when in the fall of 1873 a colporteur visited the village of San Fernando with tracts and papers from Matamoros she shared in the general voice of indignation which disturbed for some weeks the tranquillity of the village. A few books were sold, quite a number of tracts and papers given away, and for some months nothing more was seen of the *schismatic* book vender.

Quite a number of illustrated books for children were circulated and whenever Angelita saw any of these in the hands of her little playmates she warned them of the dreadful judgments the priest had said would fall on all who read them.

She was not always successful in her efforts, as she supposed to hinder a corrupt literature from being circulated in the village, but many were the praises bestowed upon her when she told her confessor how she had labored and enabled him to get track of the offenders and if possible get possession of the obnoxious papers and commit them to the flames.

Her mother's opportunity of service was interrupted by the second marriage of B...... S.... and having heard that house servants were receiving better wages in Matamoros she determined to remove thither, which took place in 1874.

She soon found a situation, but it was by separating from her children, though sometimes she could spend the nights with them.

She had rented a room near the central part of the city where her children could live quietly and where she could go to see them when any exigency required.

Angela was then about fifteen years of age, Encarnacion or Chona as she was familiarly called was about twelve, and the little boy Manuel, a restless obstreperous urchin of four years, who wore a single calico shirt, gave them a full share of anxiety and care to keep him anywhere within reasonable bounds.

Angelita frequented the Catholic Church, was instructing a class of children in the Catechism preparatory to confirmation, and when Bishop Montesdeoca came to the city, she obtained an interview, and piously knelt and kissed his hand, hoping that her soul would be much sooner released from purgatory by this act of respect to her Bishop. She was pleased to see several of her pupils receive confirmation and with great pleasure assisted the girls to adjust their white gauze veils to go and confess, so as to receive their first communion, or partake of the holy wafer, which she reverently believed to be the body and blood of Christ.

Such was her life when an unexpected incident crossed her pathway. She had been intimate in San Fernando with Petra S....sister of B....S....who kept house for her brother M....S....a merchant whose place of business was near the Market.

However he determined to reside farther from the centre of town and being well acquainted with Julian Mireles, who had gone as colporteur to San Fernando, on hearing that the room adjoining the one occupied by Julian and family and which had been recently occupied by Micajah M. Binford and wife, was vacated, he rented the room. Julian had a daughter, Gertrudis, an excellent singer, and devout Protestant and their previous acquaintance was not interrupted by a difference of religious opinion if indeed any such difference existed, for M....S....was a subscriber to "El Ramo de Olivo," and both he and his sister Petra were familiar with the reform movement inaugurated in 1861 by their uncle Ramon Lozano. They were tolerant at least, and when Gertrudis invited Petra to accompany her to the reunion or meeting of the "Friends" she gladly consented to come and was greatly pleased with the singing.

A few days afterwards her intimate friend, Angelita came to visit her and was introduced to Gertrudis and was requested by Petra to attend the Friends' meeting where she could see how their singing would compare with that of the Catholic choir of which Angelita was a well known vocalist.

A few days later Julian Mireles and family removed to a room adjoining that occupied by the three children of the widow Zúñiga.

Angelita had lost somewhat her fear of heretics, the presence of two large Protestant congregations was a fact known to all the residents, and her mother was servant in a family of foreigners who were secretly Protestants.

Thus when invited by Gertrudis she consented to accompany her to the meeting out of curiosity only. It was a beautiful night in June 1875 that with many misgivings of conscience this interesting young lady entered the spacious hall, No. 49 Calle de Bravo, occupied by the Friends' Mission, and without the least thought that she would ever enter the place again.

There was nothing attractive in the surroundings. The hall was like most buildings in Mexico, built on a line with the narrow sidewalk, and had three pair of glass doors giving ample light by day. This being a night service it was lighted by hanging lamps in the alley and wall lamps with glass reflectors. At one end of the room was a desk, and on this was a large Spanish Bible, which had recently been acquired from a preacher who passed through the city, as a large Bible had not before been seen by our missionaries.

Two preachers sat behind the desk, on the same level as the congregation, both were young men, aged respectively thirty one and twenty one years. Behind the speakers was a glass window opening to the yard; and to which the fanatical persons at times directed a throw of pieces of bricks or large beef bones to annoy the speakers and if possible interrupt the congregation. The street doors were open and oftentimes small groups of passers by stopped to listen to the services, some quiet and attentive, others boisterous and reviling. The speakers and audience were so accustomed to these inconveniences that they did not appear to be in the least disturbed by them. These were however novel scenes for the new comer, and she could not fail to note the contrast between this humble scene and the spacious naves, and heavy columns of the Catholic church edifice, with the long row of pictures and statues of the Saints on each side and the altar in front glowing with gold and tinsel, and the new chandeliers with their gaudy glow of glass prisms which had but a short time previously cost over seven hundred dollars, and had been formally *blessed* amid the showers of incense and great demonstrations of jubilee in the presence of over two thousand spectators.

Here everything was rude and simple, but the language flowed forth, not in the accustomed Latin of the Romish service but in clear words in the language of the listeners. A hymn was read by M. M. Binford, which was sung by the congregation, and followed by the reading of a chapter of the New Testament and remarks on the same, then one of the preachers knelt in prayer, followed by a brief and pointed sermon on the value of the Bible, and the duty of all men to study it diligently so as to know the will of God concerning them. The power of Christ to redeem the soul from spiritual death and give it power and life was dwelt upon, and the speaker pleaded earnestly with all who were anxious about their souls' salvation to seek the pardon of their sins through the blood of Christ, and live a new life, kept by the power of God unto salvation through faith in the only Mediator between God and man.

Angelita listened with deep feeling to these words and seemed to see how great a blessing she had been deprived of by a church which virtually prohibited her reading the Holy Scriptures. The answer of her own heart convinced her that words so fitting to her own needs must proceed from the fountain of all truth, she lost her confidence in the shadowy forms of Romanism and then and there resolved to be a Protestant.

The closing service impressed her greatly. Agustin Gonzalez who had been admitted a member at the last business meeting arose at the request of M. M. Binford and in answer to his inquiries gave a full and clear statement of his knowledge of his own sinfulness, and clear account of his conversion, of his sense of acceptance through faith in Christ. A hymn was sung at the close when the eldest speaker said very simply: "May God accompany all with his blessing as we separate." She was deeply impressed and longed for the next meeting day to come.

# CHAPTER VII.

THE next meeting was to take place on First Day afternoon, and she would have to go openly, and it would become generally known that she was an investigator of the new religion. She had a still more powerful obstacle to overcome. When she told her mother where she had been and what a good meeting they had in the Friends' Mission Room, her mother in no wise sympathised with her and at first was entirely unwilling for her to go again. Angelita however by the mediation of their neighbors gained permission to do so, and the arguments of Julian Mireles produced quite an impression on the mind of the widow Zúñiga, although she was unwilling open-ly to acknowledge it. However he gained his point so far as to induce her to send her youngest daughter and little boy to the school taught by Gulielma M. Purdie, who was assisted in the recitations by Jesus Mireles, son of Julian, and thus on the coming Sabbath Angelita had the pleasure of taking her sister with her to meeting.

The meeting was a very impressive one. It began with a Bible Class, the study of a portion of one of the Gospels, followed by a regular meeting for wor-ship and instruction. The younger children formed a separate class, and after the opening exercises with-drew to the interior porch, where they were instructed by M. M. Binford, on whom the principal services devolved during the public meeting, and it tended to confirm Angelita in her adhesion to the Protestant faith. Her sister was also deeply interested in the exercises and ready to second the determination of Angelita to whom she had long been accustomed to look for direction and instruction.

This was the beginning of an eventful week in the life of Angela Aguilar y Zúñiga. As we have already intimated Julian Mireles had earnestly set himself to seek by some means to win Francisca Zúñiga to the cause of the Gospel of Christ. He saw that her curiosity had been awakened and that whilst she was unwilling to let her daughter know it, she was half persuaded to go and hear what the foreigners had to say. Julian proposed to take her to the Presbyterian service, whilst her daughter was absent on an evening visit, and not let her know anything about it. Thus on Wednesday night at half past seven Francisca Zúñiga entered the room occupied by the Presbyterian Mission in company with Julian Mireles and wife. Both the Quaker missionaries were present and by invitation the senior one took charge of the services. Thus quite unexpectedly she had chanced to hear the very same persons to whose preaching her daughter had listened with so much attention. Although she took at that time no open stand in favor of the reform movement, all her opposition to the attendance of her daughters at meeting ceased.

The following night Angelita and her sister attended the meeting at the Friends' Mission, this time three brethren sat at the desk, one of them a veteran laborer in the reform movement, who appeared to be about fifty years of age, and who was the principal speaker on that occasion. He read a part of his discourse, now and then launching out in earnest denunciations of the errors and abominations of Romanism and the horrid persecutions they had inflicted on Protestants, not only in other countries, but quite recently in Mexico. He brought together a long list of martyrs in different epochs, closing with a touching description of the assassination of John L. Stephens at Ahualulco de Mercado, which had taken place but a few months previously, and which had filled the Liberal party with consternation.

The speaker was as we have already stated a very singular personage in every respect, for although of a dark Indian cast of countenance, he was rather tall and slender, his large black eyes seemed to betray an ancestry which terminated among the Moors of Spain, his high forehead gave him an intelligent look, whilst several protuberances which would alarm a phrenologist and which seem to have resulted from blows caused by severe accidents in mining and the attacks of his persecutors, gave him a weird aspect not altogether prepossessing. One thing however was in his favor, he was a Mexican, he spoke his native language with surprising fluency and brought out in detail those political movements and historic events connected with the long struggle for religious liberty in which he had taken an active part. He seemed to bear the whole audience along with him in his advocacy of the Reform movement.

We must bear in mind that he was of a powerful mind and had a great influence on the audience. He had arrived in the city but a few weeks previous, the well known history of his sufferings had enlisted their sympathies, and they had collected about ten dollars to aid his family, which on this occasion he acknowledged by most touching comparisons with the benevolent exertions of the early church as recorded in the Acts of the Apostles.

He made a most touching appeal to his hearers to cleanse their souls from having part in the blood of Stephens by leaving the church of Rome, and joining that movement which was in perfect harmony with the existing laws of the country, and the best interests of the people, to return to the first principles of the Gospel of Christ as found in the New Testament, the Gospel of salvation as Christ taught it, without addition or comment, the alone way to salvation. Angelita was not only fully persuaded of the truth she heard but at once anxious to clear her own soul from any acquiescence in the death of Stephens by a public withdrawal from the church of Rome and an open avowal of her adhesion to the pure Gospel of Christ.

During the same week she recceived a visit from Gulielma M. Purdie who understanding the difficul-

THE SPANISH COUNTESS.

ties she had encountered in her conversion presented her a beautiful little pamphlet entitled "*Father Ignacio and his Victims*," a deeply touching narrative of the conversion of a Spanish Countess who was burned at the stake in 1559. This tract presented in familiar converse the vast difference between the Romish worship of Saints, and particularly of the Virgin Mary and the New Testament doctrine of *One Mediator* between God and man, the man Christ Jesus, and direct access to God in prayer and a clear personal experience of the pardon of sins through the atoning blood of Christ.

The narrative of this tract opens in the beautiful home of Count Cardeña, where the mother had died and the principal care of the household rested on the eldest daughter, who had taken due care of the instruction of her younger sister. The eldest becomes anxious about her soul's welfare, for she notices the

THE GARDENER'S PRAYER.

want of perfect peace even when attentive to all the duties and penances of her church. In this mood she takes a walk in the fields and sits down by a rocky prominence to meditate on the wonders of nature and the beauties God has permitted us even in this present world. She hears a voice in earnest prayer, the words sound strange for she hears that Spain lies in darkness, and that voice asks God by the light of his Gospel to dissipate the gross darkness of error and save the nation. A moment later she is surprised as their gardener emerges from behind the rock, as surprised at being overheard in his prayer as was she in hearing him pray so earnestly to God. She finds that he possesses a copy of one of the Gospels, that he reads it daily at home to his niece, and she gladly joins them in these occasions of worship and prayer. The Inquisition tracks out the Huguenot laborer and he and his *protégée* perish in the flames. He leaves the copy of the Gospel with his wealthy convert, and that volume is blessed to the conversion of her sister, her brother is converted whilst copying one of the

E

Gospels for the monks of his convent, all meet in
the hall of torment and perish side by side in an *Auto
de Fé*. The conversations embrace every point of
difference between Romanism and Protestantism,
and it was just the tract which Angelita needed, and
was greatly useful in confirming the resolution she
had formed to break away from Rome even in face
of scorn and contempt.

This tract has passed through three editions on
our presses, the last one being stereotyped, and has
been reprinted in Toluca and Guadalajara, thus
thousands of persons have been influenced by its
clear and bold teachings. It is chiefly a translation of
a small volume entitled "The Castilian Martyrs,"
issued by the Methodist Book Concern, New York.
Some grave historical errors are corrected, for that
volume has them perish in the *Inquisition at Madrid.*

AUTO DE FÉ, IN SEVILLE.

There were then but two
Inquisitions in Spain, one at
*Valladolid* and the other at
*Seville*, where the family
whose martyrdom forms the
basis of the volume really
suffered. Juan Gonzalez and
his two sisters were tied to
three stakes and began singing a Psalm whilst the flames
wrapped their youthful forms
until their souls took their flight from the burning
tenement to form part in the heavenly throng which
John saw of *witnesses*, who having been faithful unto
death have received a crown of life.

To many of our readers any mention of the Inquisition would seem a needless reviving of records of
deeds which history condemns, but *we* who have felt
more or less the unchanged tenor of Romanism in
Spanish countries, and have been called upon to
record in our pages deeds of blood, when whole

congregations have been almost annihilated by armed mobs headed by priests, where in one case a minister was shot by the priest who led the mob, a foreign missionary being the first martyr, to us Rome is still the *Mystery Babylon*, stained with the blood of the martyrs.

Yet this blood of the martyrs is the seed of the church, and no epoch of the work has been more fruitful to the cause than that immediately following the death of John Luther Stephens. At the sight of the mangled corpse weltering in blood, the wife of his native co-laborer whose life was providentially saved, and who was still a firm Catholic, throwing her arms around her husband's neck exclaimed: "Oh my child! I was unwilling to believe that Catholicism was a persecuting religion as thou didst tell me; I believed as my relatives told me that the Catholic religion was to be 'persecuted but not overcome,' but now I am undeceived. Was it necessary that I should see *this* in order to be convinced? We can no longer remain members of a church stained with blood and infamy."

It may be interesting to know that one of those who took an active part in the mob which assassinated Stephens and sought the life of his co-laborer Severiano Gallegos, our peace poet, is now like him, a Methodist preacher. They recently met at Conference. Whilst the recent convert was preaching he saw Gallegos seated among the preachers, and stopping his discourse threw his arms around him, asking his forgiveness for the rash attempt upon his life, and thanked God for having frustrated his wicked design.

In the midst of such persecutions, and beholding around us the criminal conduct of priests, such as would stain our pages by their recital, when not only are the living hunted like wild beasts, but in one case a dead body is scourged to cleanse the soul of its former occupant from the crime of having taken an affirmation to sustain and defend the Constitution and Reform Laws of Mexico, in the midst of such events we feel bound to handle Romanism as William Penn handles it in his "Seasonable Caveat against Popery," as it ever will be handled by those who know its true character, and can trace the unchanging leopard spots beneath whatever enticing outward fleece they may be hidden.

It need scarcely surprise us that in view of these things a very large number of people should abandon Romanism, and knowing no other religion should fall into infidelity. To such an extent has this been the case that a city paper printed in the capital of the State of Tabasco said of the attendance at services there during the Holy Week: "The priest walks solitary and alone under the arches of the cathedral, the unbelieving multitude have fled from the altar, and only in the isolated villages are religious services attended or appreciated."

The reason of this apostasy is clearly set forth by Joaquin Chiriboga in his *"La Luz del Pueblo:"* "Faith and philanthropic sentiments have disappeared from the world because piety and good sense have fled from the church. The discourses of the Pontiff, the decisions of the Councils and the pastorals of the Bishops clash with that charity and right reason which should ever accompany the inspirations of those who call themselves the vicars and ministers of Jesus Christ, and from this results that chaos of errors and selfish passions in which Catholic nations are submerged."

# CHAPTER VIII.

OPENLY EMBRACES PROTESTANTISM. IS ADMITTED A
MEMBER OF FRIENDS' SOCIETY. GENERAL VIEW OF
THE MEXICAN MISSION IN 1875. NEW DIFFICULTIES.

E have now arrived at a point from whence the
records of the business meeting will enable us
to fix the dates and bring the events into historical order. The following Sabbath was a
memorable day in the life of Angelita. It was then
that she made known her convictions and her resolution to openly throw aside all allegiance to Rome and
publicly declare herself a Protestant.

It was a severe trial, for she was naturally timid,
and she knew this step would sever many ties with
former associates, and would bring upon her both
ridicule and persecution. It would also place her
in care of new spiritual advisers, who were almost
strangers to her, for she had first met them only
three weeks previously. It is true that one thing
made her feel less diffident. In receiving counsel, and
as she had formerly believed forgiveness of sins from
her confessor, she was obliged to be alone with an
unmarried man, and the sad tales of the abuse of
these opportunities for leading young females astray
had filled her with anxiety, whilst those who were
now to give her counsel and caution were both
married men, and their wives sat with her during the
meeting, and there was a certain nearness of social
feeling she never could have felt toward the priests.

There was no seclusion, when her request had been made known through the kindness of Mariana Villa-nueva de Mireles, she was requested to remain after the meeting was dismissed, and whilst the audience was separating M. M. Binford went to where she was seated and began to inquire about the state of her own soul and her experience of forgiveness of sins and hope of eternal life through the atonement of Christ. Also of her conversion from the supersti-tions of Romanism to the free and full Gospel of Christ. Her answers were clear and decisive. She believed herself to be a child of God through faith in the sacrifice of Christ, and was determined by the promised grace of God to bring her life into full con-formity with the teachings of Jesus Christ and his Apostles as found in the New Testament. In her sister there was not that clearness and depth of ex-perience, yet there was a full acceptance of the teachings of Christ, and faith in him as her only Savior. She was fully prepared to second the move-ment of her sister and henceforth be one with her in Christian faith.

So soon as the writer had attended to the distri-bution of some papers to the dispersing assembly he joined M. M. Binford in his conversation with the young converts, and both being satisfied it was deci-ded to propose them to the next business meeting for admission as members, together with another person whose name is not mentioned.

This was the last meeting our Friend M. M. Binford attended before embarking for the United States, for a brief journey as was then supposed but which finally resulted in his being unable to rejoin the mission during the eight years which have elapsed since that favored Sabbath evening.

There was a feeling of sorrow at the brief separa-tion of one whose pastoral gift had been abundantly blessed to many souls, and had it been thought that this was to be a long separation (we will still hope it may not be a final parting,) the sorrow would have been unbounded.

The mission at that time was sadly in need of funds, and aside from the broken health of his wife it was thought that a visit to different places would enable our Friend to lay the subject before Friends at home and save the mission. In this respect the results were most gratifying and the work not only continued but considerably enlarged. Indiana Yearly Meeting appropriated $1500, and quite a large sum was collected in Baltimore, Philadelphia and New York.

Little did the congregation think that in a few weeks they would have to part with another laborer, the veteran colporteur and evangelist Clemente A. Vivero, who accepted a solicitation from the Methodist superintendent of Western Texas and was soon after stationed at Rio Grande City, about 100 miles farther up the river, and on the American side.

But a few months later they were to bid farewell to their only remaining minister under most unfavorable and unpromising circumstances. But we must not press forward too rapidly. By examining the record of the business meeting we find that in the seventh session, held on the 7th of 8th Month or August 1875; "This session was opened by reading the minutes of the preceding session, after which the treasurer informed the meeting that $2.50 had been collected during the month for aiding the sick and poor members, and he was directed to apply it to the same use as that of the previous session.* The brother who presides, Samuel A. Purdie, then presented the names of three persons who were desirous of joining as members, having been examined according to our Discipline, they are now admitted as members of this

---

* To aid the family of Clemente Abraham Vivero.

Society, on making the public profession of their faith, and acceptance of the Gospel of Christ as their rule of life and conduct. The committee of beneficence (overseers of the poor,) in the fulfillment of their commission reported that there had been no sickness during the month, and that Cástulo Salas desires to be united in membership with our Society. Agustin Gonzalez was appointed to fill the commission of beneficence during the present month.

JESUS MIRELES, *Secy.*"

The minute does not mention the names of those admitted, and appears to have been an intentional omission, rectified by concurrent testimony and by being the only case where blank spaces were left in place of names.

As this session was held on the 7th we find that the following day was the time when these two sisters made the public profession called for in the minute. It was a series of questioning very similar to that already mentioned, and took place in the presence of the whole assembly in the regular meeting for worship, which in this case was on First-day evening, the new members simply rising at their seats so that all present, not only members and believers but unbelievers could thus feel the force of their testimony for Jesus.

We might here state that often this plain testimony had a more convincing effect than the preaching of the Gospel, because they could well understand how much self sacrifice it cost these timid converts to thus openly break off old companionships and stand up for Jesus, not only before a frowning world, but also before a powerful and persecuting church. Aside from the converting power of such a public profession, or as the Spanish people call it confession, on the audience it had a most beneficial effect on the new converts themselves. It was a decided step of separation from the world, and from the Catholic church as well. They were strengthened by the Savior's promise:— " Whosoever therefore shall confess me before men, him will I confess also before my Father which is in heaven." Mat. x. 32.

They were however fully reminded that a verbal confession is vain unless the child of God shows forth in a Christain life and conversation the fruits meet for repentance, thus forming an epistle known and read of all men. These were days of much reviling, crowds of rough looking people thronged our doors and many means were employed for disturbing the gatherings, yet we may look upon this as a great blessing, for making it so severe a trial to profess the truth it cleared us of an element moved only by popular favor, who might otherwise have sided with us without actual conversion.

Aside from these trials an unexpectedly dark cloud broke over the young sisters who had now joined us, Their mother had become tolerant, and acquiesced in the change, but a sudden estrangement broke upon Angelita from the very persons who had been the first to encourage her change of position. Respect for the dead and love for the living induce us to throw the vail of silence over those events which whilst proving the faith of the young convert, induced her to stand for the right, cost what it might. She determined hastily to change her home, and in the emergency was obliged to take up her abode in a much humbler residence than the one she was resolved to leave.

AT HOME IN THE WORK.

Hierogliphic names of each day of the month.

FROM THE AZTEC CALENDER.

# CHAPTER IX.

THE DARKEST HOUR BEFORE DAWN. BECOMES AN IN-
MATE OF THE MISSION FAMILY. FIRST EFFORTS TO
INTEREST THE CHILDREN IN GOSPEL HYMNS.

ON Ninth Street, between Bravo and Matamoros,
some poor man had thrown a roof over the inter-
vening space between two humble dwellings and
closed it at front and rear, so as to afford a shelter
which served for a shop. The roof was of inch boards
with narrow battens, and having but a slight incline
was but little protection against the rains. As no
severe rain had fallen for a long interval of time the
ground beneath was now dry, and as it was offered
for rent at two dollars per month she decided to
occupy it. Under the cover of night they took their
baggage and moved to the new place. The three
orphans in a single journey on foot took all their
goods to their new home.

Nature seemed to partake of the same dark aspect as their surrounding circumstances. It was a cloudy night and now and then bright chains of lightning illuminated the northern horizon, accompanied by low sullen rolls of thunder, and as the young girl reflected on the sudden change she found it impossible to sleep.

She had peace of mind in the thought that she had taken the right course, that she had decided not to be a hearer only of the Gospel, but a doer thereof. Strange as it may seem that very night a deluging rain broke upon the city and before day dawned the ground of their floor was so moistened that on stepping about it at once became reduced to a soft and plastic mud.

The little barefoot boy could however go to the market and buy eatables, so she gave him the last quarter she had and sent him to buy some things for breakfast and bring back the change. He went along the narrow brick side-walk and boy like carelessly tripping along let fall the quarter, which disappeared in the bottom of a mud-hole formed by the rain of the previous night and if ever found, it certainly never returned to its rightful owners. With a muddy floor, and no chimney, without coal and bankrupt, such was the mournful aspect of the new day as it opened upon this sorrowful group of children. Her mother had drawn all her pay but a few days before and now there seemed no recourse left but in some unlooked for interposition of God's Providence.

These sudden and severe changes had wrought on her naturally susceptible temperament and she found that aside from hunger, which she not only had to suffer herself, and saw no way to abate the doleful pleadings of her little brother, but she felt feverish and after sending her brother and sister to school she lay down utterly exhausted. During the forenoon the countenance of little Manuel bore unmistakable evidence of some misfortune having crossed his pathway, and this induced Gulielma to question him closely as to the cause of his tears, and notwithstanding the efforts of Encarnacion to prevent his revealing their financial status he had no better thought than to tell it in full.

No sooner had Gulielma comprehended their needs than she sent some aid from the meeting's treasury, which they considered a great favor, and thus they were only obliged to fast half a day.

The following day Angelita found her fever increasing and Gulielma at once saw that the rains would soon render their hovel very unhealthy and perhaps imperil their lives, and therefore requested Angelita to come and stay with her until she should recover, and she would also take care of her brother and sister meanwhile.

Angelita was removed to an airy bed room at one end of our porch and the other two accommodated in the kitchen in the yard. It was expected that this change would be temporary, and that so soon as Angelita should recover, some appropriate room could be secured and they could again keep house by themselves. Her symptoms became more serious and large red spots on the skin made us fear that she had been taken with small-pox, which had caused several deaths among our members.

This however proved to be only a variety of fever which was of but a few days' duration, and the change from a muddy hovel to an airy room with a plank floor had been as useful as medicine in hastening her recovery. The days of her illness had brought her into intimate relations with Gulielma and the bond of sympathy seemed to increase from day to day, and so soon as she could be up about the room she used every effort to repay the kind attentions she had received during her illness. Gulielma felt the need of some such sympathizing companion to aid

her in her household cares, and thus what was
supposed to be a brief change for recovery grew into
a deep and lasting bond of affection which was not
severed even by her subsequent marriage, though
thenceforth she had her home elsewhere. Her residence in the mission family was a school of usefulness and notwithstanding her limited education, was
wonderfully improved by her and fitted her for that
position which she afterwards filled in the Church
of Christ.

She grew in grace rapidly and began to accompany
Gulielma in her visits to our members to give them
counsel and encouragement, and to reconcile differ-
ences and promote a harmonious co-operation in the
Lord's work.

It was customary at that time on noting the
absence of any member from our meeting on
First-day afternoon to go immediately after meeting
to see if they were sick, or ascertain the reason of
their absence. Thus the physical and moral status
of the little circle was closely watched and the company were brought into near fellowship and earnestness of purpose in the prosecution of the work of
evangelization.

Angelita was an excellent singer and aided the
mission very materially in teaching the children
to sing, and thus early train their minds to a grate-
ful remembrance of the many benefits their Heavenly
Father has conferred upon them in the Gospel of
Christ.

About an hour was spent each day in this most
useful exercise, which served to attract the children,
and train their voices, as well as impress them with
a sense of their privileges and responsiblities. Now
and then some travelling member of some of our
sister churches or some loving sisters from the
American congregations of Brownsville, Texas, would
take due care to enable her to acquire the tune of

some new translation of our familiar Gospel hymns which by nearly every mail came from the pen of Thomas M. Westrup, who has done more perhaps than any other missionary to place Gospel truth in the sweet language of song before the evangelical Christians of Spanish America. The little hymn book of 16 pages grew by these additions very rapidly and thus not only our own but other churches were supplied through our press.

To give our readers an idea of the transformation wrought in English hymns when adapted to Spanish verse we present the following interlineal rendering of one strofa of the well known hymn beginning,

"WHEN I CAN READ MY TITLE CLEAR."

i Cuando veo claro el título
　　When　　I see　clear　　the title

Que me asegura los cielos,
Which me　secures　the heavens,

Digo adios á mis recelos,
I say adieu to　my　　fears,

Dejo al punto de llorar.
I leave the . point　of Weeping.

This specimen will suffice to show that they are rather *imitations* than *translations*. Below is a miniature of the first page of our hymn book.

LIRA EVANGELICA.

CÁNTICO 1?

_1_

Aqui juntos reunidos
Alabémosle, Señor,
A tus hijos muy queri os
Les concedes este honor;
Adorarte y a'al arte
Sea nuestra ocupacion
Que podamos proclamart· } bla
Dios de nuestra salvacion. }

_2_

Siempre seas alaba o
Por tu inmensa caridad,
¡Oh gran Dios y eel lindo
Seas en la eternidad.
Tú, Señor, eres benigno;
Tú perdonas con amor. 
Le tus hijos tu eres digno } bh
De recibir el loor.　}
　　　　L. 8.

TROPICAL LOWLANDS OF SOUTHERN TAMAULIPAS.

# CHAPTER X.

FULLER ORGANIZATION OF THE NATIVE CHURCH, AND
ABSENCE OF THEIR PASTOR. HOW THE MEETINGS
WERE CONDUCTED. DARKENING POLITICAL CLOUDS.

THE business meeting held on the 5th of September was a noteworthy one. During the preceding month Clemente A. Vivero had removed to Corpus Christi, Texas where he was to preach until the meeting of the Annual Conference at San Antonio, and the church at Matamoros felt under obligations to give him a letter of recommendation. This letter was signed by all the members who were present and was the outgrowth of their fervent desires to aid in helping this eccentric but in many ways extraordinary man in his Gospel labors. He went in company with Alejo Hernandez who had also been a very successful evangelist of the Methodist Episcopal Church in Texas, but had been transferred to the care of the new church opened in the city of Mexico. He had become paralytic and had been stopping in Matamoros for some months hoping for relief from the able physicians of this city, but becoming worse he returned to Corpus Christi where he had founded the meeting, and died there twelve days after reaching the place.

One of the earliest converts under the labors of our Mission was a Frenchman, who had been a strict Romanist, and from curiosity came to our earliest meetings, but being very clearly impressed with the

Truth he embraced it with earnestness and took quite an active part in our business meetings. He had noticed that the frequent changes in the *Junta de Beneficencia*, were rather prejudicial than otherwise and by reading in the Acts of the Apostles found that they called those appointed to this work *deacons* and seemed to have made no limitation of time of service. He proposed that this change be made and the church be thus more perfectly made a reproduction of the apostolic church. The members at once took the matter into serious and prayerful deliberation, several passages of the New Testament touching upon the duties and qualifications of those appointed to official stations in the early church were considered: and then the meeting decided that being a matter of considerable importance and requiring much care in the selection of the proper person or persons to fill these stations permanently it would be best to leave the matter open until next meeting.

In the meeting held October 4th, 1875 the proposition of Bernardo de Lapuyade was again very prayerfully considered and as it was also deemed necessary for the deacon or deacons to co-operate with the minister in the pastoral care of the flock, the members had fixed their attention on the qualifications of Agustin Gonzalez and he was appointed six months on trial, and if the church then deemed best was to be considered permanently appointed. At this second meeting the necessity of appointing elders to co-operate with the minister and deacon in the care of the flock was brought forward. These appointments were urged upon the attention of the meeting more particularly by the ill health of their pastor.

I had suffered a severe attack of pneumonia the preceding winter and thus the delicate condition of my lungs had by the constant exercise in preaching so as to be heard clearly by the crowds gathering near our doors and windows, given rise to a severe attack of asthma, and it seemed evident that rest and absence from this region of sudden and violent atmospheric changes would be necessary, and the young flock remain without a preacher. The appointment of elders was left for consideration for another month, when Pedro de los Santos and Jesus Valdez were appointed for six months, it being a very general opinion that there were at that time no persons sufficiently mature in their religious experience to be appointed permanently as elders of the flock.

Thus did the little church arrange with due care and in the reverent fear of the Lord, to work together for mutual edification during the absence of one whom they had looked upon as their instructor in the Gospel of Christ.

A letter of recommendation to the pastors of other evangelical churches and also to the people at large was prepared by the clerk, Jesus Mireles, and signed by nearly all the members of our meeting. We had at that time but few members who could not read and write, and we have not been able to make much progress among the more ignorant and debased class of people. It is the investigating class of people, whose minds have loosed the moorings which bound them to the blind creed of Rome, who have been most ready to receive Gospel in this land.

Whilst the tender interest of the members of the little church had thus made provision for the care and instruction of the flock, the welfare of Gulielma was to be taken into consideration, and Angelita became more than ever her bosom friend and co-laborer in the household and in the work of the church.

. The meetings were kept up in my absence, the exercises consisting chiefly of the reading of Scripture passages and expositions, mostly from printed works, the exercises of prayer being mostly by Jesus Mireles and Agustin Gonzalez.

The reader will pardon a digression, and be ready
to follow me in a hurried sketch of my journey.

There was at that time no line of steamers engaged
in the coasting trade, which was limited to supplying
Matamoros with tropical fruits. There were two
vessels making occasional trips, and on one of these,

"*Los Tres Hermanos*," of 16 tons
burden, and drawing about two
feet eight inches of water, I had
the rare good fortune to secure a
passage to Tampico. We raised
anchor, or rather loosed our roping from a point known as "*El
Muelle*," "The Wharf," though
nothing marked the site but the name, and that was
wanting. We were three days descending the Rio
Grande to Bagdad, a land distance of 32 miles, but
by the river channel three times that distance. Here
our little craft was detained four days by contrary
winds, when we were able to cross the bar and
began our voyage over the rough waves of winter on
the Gulf of Mexico. This was on the 22d of December
1875, and we were six days in running down the
coast to Tampico, though in a favorable time the
journey is made in 48 hours. The weather was
beautiful, but the wind was contrary, and the sea
voyage worked wonders in restoring my broken
health.

The day I had left Matamoros, a native helper of
the Presbyterian Church (North) had left Mexico
city for Tampico, and the day we crossed the bar at
Bagdad his steamship left the wharf at Veracruz.
He reached Tampico five days before us.

On this journey I was accompanied by Calixto
Lara as colporteur, and as we had a large supply of
books and tracts, although my chief object was
the restoration of my health, yet we were prepared
for active work in extending the Gospel. Our col-

porteur was sustained by Friends of Baltimore Yearly Meeting. This journey laid in some measure the foundation for the great work since accomplished by our Southern Mission.

So soon as the place of worship was arranged, I joined Pedro Trujillo, the native helper, in opening meetings, and thus my whole stay in that city was an active effort to aid in laying the foundation of the mission now sustained in that port by the Associated Reformed Presbyterian Church.

Near the city of Tampico are the ruins of several cities pertaining to the ancient Huastec kingdom, and I had hoped to visit them and collect some of the interesting specimens of antiquity which abound among the debris of their ruined pyramids.

Early one morning we entered a canoe and began running up the Tamesí river, intending to land at Altamira. Our canoe seemed to open its way amid the countless multitudes of water fowl which were wintering in this delightful region, the banks were studded with tropical verdure, abounding in gay flowers, whilst birds quite as brilliant in color were flitting about amid the dense verdure.

On the way we stopped at a ranch where we hired horses and a guide in order to visit the ruins on Sierra de la Palma, 27 miles from Altamira. Our guide swam his horses across the river and went by land to meet us at Tancol where we were to pass the night. The day had been cold, a brisk north wind was blowing, and a chilly rain·kept us saturated, thus we passed the night without bedding, in a reed hut which had never been plastered, and we awoke next morning with a burning tropical fever, and had to abandon our journey and return to Tampico for medical treatment. I had especially hoped to obtain some of the small clay idols which abound in these ruins, and which are so thoroughly burned that 300 to 500 years of exposure to the moist tropical soil and the shade of tropical vegetation have not injured them in the least. On my return to Tampico a pious Christian lady who was interested in my remaining as long as possible in the city in order to help in the good work, presented me with one of these idols in order to remove all desire to visit the ruins. This idol is now in the cabinet of Earlham College, at Richmond Ind. The accompanying cut represents one of the most perfect specimens yet found and is in the collection of Alejandro Prieto, the historian. With the exception of the shortness of the forearm the figure is pretty well proportioned. There is quite a diversity of opinion among antiquarians as to the true nature of these clay images. Some are inclined to look upon them as symbolical mementoes of the person in

HUASTEC CLAY IMAGE.

whose grave they had been interred. These clay images are found in the places of interment, which were orderly in their arrangement and decoration.

These were but a trifle larger than our cut, and must not be confounded with the massive stone idols which were placed on the summits of their pyramids. I saw two of the latter in Tampico, but was not inclined to purchase or pay freight on them. One of the latter class is represented at the close of this chapter. It was whilst engaged in these investigations that I prepared my "Child's History of Mexico," a work which has been abundantly useful in combating idolatry in all its forms, aside from its utility as a text book for schools. About 5,000 copies have been put into circulation.

The darkening political clouds, and the news that Gen. Porfirio Diaz, who had escaped from the country, was at Brownsville, Texas, made me hasten home at once, as Matamoros would be the probable point of attack, and I was desirous of joining my wife and the little church in the hour of trial.

MEXICAN STONE IDOL.

Sculptured Rock, showing flathead type of Itza and Huastec Images.

# CHAPTER XI.

WE will take a glance at the household in Matamoros in the latter part of February 1876. The
mails had failed to bring for some days any
tidings of the absent one, and the impression
left by the last letters was that I would embark on
the first sloop up the coast. News had reached the
city that the "Alba" of 19 tons burden, loaded with

300 bunches of bananas, 50 pine
apples and seven passengers, had
left Tampico for Matamoros, but
had failed to reach her destination,
the anxiety led to rumors and it
was noised abroad that she had
been shipwrecked. It is quite probable that the light-house keeper at

Homeward bound on the "Alba."

the mouth of the Pánuco river had seen us driven
past by a furious gale which it seemed impossible
for such a craft to survive. We had been obliged to
seek safety in the roads to the leeward of Lobos Island,
near Cape Roxo, where the coral reefs permitted us
to anchor in safety.

Gulielma had not given way to undue alarm, and
waited patiently for further news.

It was noon of a most beautiful day, the 28 th of
February, and the prairies around the city were now

73

covered with immense beds of verbenas, whilst a beautiful pink flower seemed to rival the former in abundance and beauty.

Gulielma had made a call on most of our members that morning, and had invited the girls and young ladies to accompany her in the afternoon, in a walk outside the city walls, to enjoy the fresh breeze of the plains, and the invigorating view of the spring flowers.

At noon the owner of the buildings, who kept a hotel down town, called in to inform her that the missing sloop had reached Bagdad, that her husband was on board, and that most of the passengers had already reached the city, and that I might arrive at any moment.

Soon a dozen or more of the young ladies and school girls had gathered for the picnic, and on hearing the report there was a division of sentiment, some thinking it true, and others that it was a flying rumor, and so about half of the company went to cull flowers on the plains, whilst the others remained with Gulielma, awaiting my arrival.

The sun was fast sinking in the western horizon, the party had become tired of rambling over the plains and had just arrived under the back porch, Gulielma was entering the sitting room to arrange the repast which they had intended to partake in the shade of the mesquite trees on the prairie, when we both entered the same room by opposite doors, and the whole circle was aroused, and the simple feast was mingled with the unbounded joy of so happy and scarcely expected an occurrence.

The girls soon hurried home to tell their parents, and nearly all the members of the meeting called in before bed-time to welcome back their pastor, rejoiced at his greatly improved health.

The girls' school was re-opened and Angelita became associated with Gulielma in its management, and later in the season became its teacher. A few small boys were admitted, being all that there were at that time of the children of our members.

The threatening political clouds did not delay in gathering, and on the 2d of March, only three days after my return, Matamoros was declared to be in a state of siege, and no one was allowed to leave the city without a passport. Gen. Diaz remained in Brownsville, and whether there was any organized forces on the plains west of the city or not was the subject of most contradictory reports. It is true that a merchant of Brownsville, who had been virtually banished from Mexico for his participation in the Empire of Maximilian, had organized a squad of men, who soon after took the little village of Reynosa and after levying a forced loan on the inhabitants had approached Matamoros. At Palo Blanco they had been met by Gen. Diaz who there reformed the plan of his proposed revolution, but a difference of opinion led to the withdrawal of the merchant who had headed the adventurers up to that time.

It was now known that Gen. Diaz had obtained a loan and that he was giving his troops 50 cents per day, thus many of the poor people out of employment began crossing to Brownsville, from whence they could pass over to the revolutionary party, who were engaged in smuggling arms and ammunition across the river some miles above Brownsville. The reports as to the number of troops thus organized were so contradictory that no reliance could be placed on the current rumors. The National Guards, or state militia, were mustered and kept in order, whilst active preparations were carried on by Gen. La Barra for the defense of the city, the cannons were placed on the earthworks which surround the city on the west and south, and there seemed no doubt but that the government troops within the city were too numerous and well drilled to expect an early attack.

Some reports placed the outside party at 300 and others at 500, whilst the government troops of infantry, artillery and cavalry were about 700 strong, and the city troops or National Guard consisted of 1,000 men.

Yet on March 31st at a little before sunset a reconnoitering force of 150 men, headed by General Diaz made a feint of attack, and filled the city with consternation, the stores being closed and doors barred awaiting the struggle. After taking a distant view of the earthworks these forces retired and order was restored, the stores opened again the same night, and Saturday, April 1st was passed without any alarm, the foreign residents had not been warned to leave the city and it was apparent that no immediate attack was expected.

Sabbath morning, April 2d, was a beautiful sunny morning, all was quiet, the city was now void of fear, the conflicting reports were not relied upon, and the mustering of the inside forces with the ostensible object of scouring the plain and driving away the enemy, had scarcely been noticed by the people in general. We had just done breakfast when one of our elderly members called for a few minutes, and as he was about to leave I asked him what was the news, and he said that it was rumored that the outside party would attack the city that day. As he left we accompanied him to the street door, and were still looking out on the street where he had turned the first corner, when suddenly the clash of closing doors resounded like rolling thunder all around us. We were looking westward toward the Monterey gate, when in the dim distance amid the thick clouds of dust we could discern the cavalry rushing down our street with drawn arms, whilst a shower of balls went hissing down the street. So sudden had been the attack, and so unintelligible the *confused noise of war*, that in the few moments we had been standing in the door-way Col. Parrat of the inside cavalry had reached the corner of the street, not 40 feet from us, and having already lost his hat, whirled his horse two or three times around, uncertain which street to take for safety. He finally took the north end of Ninth Street for Santa Cruz, and we having fully comprehended our situation, closed the door and running out at our back door, crossed the yard to our printing office, a small brick structure on Ninth Street. We had scarcely reached this place of greater safety when the troops of Gen. Diaz came past the office with drawn swords, fighting back the government troops, the terrible noise of clashing arms and the discharge of musketry being only separated from us by the inch doors and delicate window shutters.

We withdrew to the back room of the printing office and took our position where brick walls would intercept the balls, and waited with almost breathless anxiety the termination of the struggle. The company consisted of the widow Aguilar and her three children, my wife and an orphan girl of eight years, and our pressman and myself.

It was not so much our own peril as the thought of the carnage in the streets, and a deep sympathy with the sufferings necessarily incident to the storming of the city. Gulielma fainted twice, and suffered from chills produced by fear, from which she did not recover for some months, The others were nearly as much frightened, and the trial and anxiety of that hour and a half of suspense will never be forgotten by any one of our trembling little group. The noise finally ceased and soon the bell of the Catholic Church sounded forth the note of victory, victory to the forces of Gen, Diaz, but told us that our city had surrendered. We had not even bolted the doors of our residence and meeting rooms at No. 49 Calle de Bravo and as the thin wooden structure was very insecure we expected that what valuables we had would either be stolen by the troops, or by the city thieves who would take advantage of the disorder to steal with impunity.

We had just reached the **back** porch of our rooms, and were entering a bed room at one end of the porch when we heard the sudden blow of a ball, which entered the room at the opposite side and passing through a framed photograph, splintering the glass into fragments, struck the opposite wall from which it took a rebound and fell on the bed only three feet from us, throwing splinters from both walls over our heads, through the open door-way. Almost simultaneous was the noise of a full discharge in line from both contending forces, followed in a few moments by the deafening roar of artillery. The bell of victory had been premature, the more faithful troops having taken refuge in the powder magazine, where they made a most determined resistance for over an hour, to a deadly fire of grape and canister at close range.

With the first discharge we rushed into the main building, the walls being of two inch plank, and throwing our straw bed against the wall as an additional protection, lay down on the floor awaiting the end of the struggle. The dull thud of spent balls and the deep roar of artillery were more terrible than the first onslaught, but there was relief in a mysterious adaptability which in a measure destroys fear, by a surplus of fear, I might say a physical insensibility to danger, such as the soldiers speak of feeling when in battle, akin to that of Dr. Livingstone when shaken by the South African lion. I had experienced a similar feeling when the wild waves washed the deck of the "Alba," and partially dismantled we were hourly expecting a watery grave.

It was not valor, though the latter had led us to stand by our flock in that hour. Valor is only possible when the mind is in its normal state. In the rush of battle and amid the clamor and anguish of the suffering victims, pallor marks the face even of the boldest, and this insensibility to danger alone makes it possible for men to stand in the deadly combat; the same feeling overpowers the humblest resident, as his house seems the centre of danger, and he knows not what a moment may bring forth.

The bell again sounded forth the note of victory, the streets became quiet, in fact they seemed deserted, and some time elapsed ere the doors and windows were opened and people began to look out upon the street. When we did so, we saw a boy ride past on a beautiful horse, which was bleeding from a ghastly wound in the thigh, one of the incidents in the confusion of the hour.

That afternoon a small company gathered at the usual hour, to thank God for his watchful care over them and their families in that trying hour.

Gen. Diaz was aware that any delay would be likely to bring upon him an overpowering force, and determined at once to march upon Monterey. He determined to take the National Guard (militia) as infantry, and what troops had surrendered, and hasten forward. The National Guard consisted of undrilled troops, and having taken a route very scantily supplied with water, sun-stroke and thirst soon thinned their ranks, and finding that he would be obliged to avoid the enemy, he sent the infantry back as it was an impediment to his march.

We shall never forget the day these troops left the city, and the wives, sisters and mothers of the conscripts grouped along the street to take what might be last look at their dear ones, who were not permitted to take a formal parting from their families. The voice of plaintive wailing resounded from house to house, and many who had thus lost their only support, had not even food for a single day, and could expect nothing until a final victory should be attained, and few if any were ever to receive any compensation whatever. Hundreds of families were thus thrown into the jaws of famine, eking out a miserable existence in the most menial services.

In a few weeks those conscripts who did not perish from thirst, had either crossed over into Texas as deserters, or had returned in disorder to Matamoros. Efforts were made by Gen. Manuel Gonzalez * for the city's defense, forced loans were levied, the earth-works were being placed in order, laborers were pressed to work on the fortifications and we were expecting soon all the horrors of a bombardment, as Gen. Escobedo who led the government troops had heavy artillery with him, and Gen. Diaz who had avoided his march and had hastened to attack Gen. Fuero, had been defeated and his troops dispersed at the battle of Hicamole.

During all this time our day school was kept up, the meetings were usually attended by all or nearly all of our members, thus our permanence among them in the hour of trial and danger, and our counsels to them to avoid being drawn into the current of political events, gave as a result an increase in number and a closer union of the body. Only one member had been conscripted, and he was never engaged in actual combat, whilst but one accepted a position in the Custom House under the Diaz government.

* Now, 1883, President of Mexico.

Mexican Ensign.

# CHAPTER XIII.

OCCUPATION OF THE CITY BY GEN. ESCOBEDO. PRO-
LONGED SIEGE, WITH THE HISTORY OF THE MISSION
CHURCH DURING THE SUMMER OF 1876.

ROM day to day the alarm grew more intense,
and the fears of bombardment became more
imminent, so that every effort was made to
prepare for the defense of the city. It was in this
state of dread that the people of Matamoros retired
to rest on the night of the 16th of May, entirely
ignorant of the plan devised by Gen. Gonzalez, and
when we arose in the morning, to behold the street
lamps still burning, it was some time ere we could
believe that at 3 A. M., Gen. Gonzalez had evacuated
the city, taking with him not only the National
Guards but also the police force and night watchmen,
so that we were without any of the ordinary means
of public security. Gen. Gonzalez had requested the
foreign ambassadors to care for the peace and order
of the city, and after thousands of dollars had been
spent in repairing the earthworks and deepening the
trench to protect the city, full arrangements were
made for the peaceful entry of Gen. Escobedo, with
his army of 3,000 men, and heavy pieces of artillery.
All the arms and munitions of war were taken by
Gen. Gonzalez who marched toward San Fernando.
During the day of the 17th the City Fathers were
called together, not now the public officers, but the

81                                    G

merchants, lawyers and professional men, who were
to form the Public Security, each store was to furnish
one clerk, mounted on horseback, as a patrol, to take
the place of the police and night watchmen. This
last resort of government knows no nationality, most
of the merchants being foreigners, as also the clerks
who formed the patrol. This form of government
needed no treasury, as the quota of each store was in
mounted clerks, who were supposed to represent and
protect the property of their employers in common
and in combination with their fellow citizens. It would
seem however that among troops, police, watchmen
and deserters, all the bad people had left the city, and
no act of violence or robbery took place during the
brief and patriarchal rule of the Public Security.

As we have already stated only one of our members
had been conscripted and one had accepted a position
in the Custom House, and both of these now crossed
over to Brownsville, and remained there until the close
of the war. The remainder of our members kept aloof
from the revolution and quietly followed their usual
avocations without interruption. This was mainly due
to our teaching the peaceable nature of the Gospel
of Christ, that his kingdom is not of this world, and
therefore his servants cannot fight with carnal
weapons. Another mission established on the frontier
taught the same truth under many qualifying terms,
its pastor was absent collecting funds to assist in
building a chapel, one native helper was also absent
for his health, and the church was under the direction
of another native helper, and the elders and deacons.
All of these were drawn into the tide of political
ebullition, one of the deacons was sergeant, one of the
elders accepted a commission as colonel and the
preacher presented his name for a captain's commission, another elder had become accomplice in the
desertion of his son, thus when Gen. Escobedo
came along all of these had to take refuge in

Texas and thus all the work was suspended until the other native helper could return, and but little could be done until the establishment of peace in February of the following year permitted the return of the church officials to their homes, so as to resume their duties in the care and oversight of the church. This is an evidence of the practical working of peace principles in so warlike country as Mexico had been up to that date.

The day school continued in care of Angelita, who usually opened the school with prayer, and aside from the Catechism lesson she was very useful in teaching her pupils by a direct application of Bible truths. On noticeing this unfolding of a gift which might make her greatly useful to the church, I determined to translate and issue the Journal of Jane Hoskens, which is full of such humble aspirations to be led by the hand of the Lord in his service, that it would be greatly useful to her in this period of small service in the Master's cause. This work was warmly appreciated by the Methodist missionaries, who aided greatly in its circulation.

Angelita accompanied Gulielma in her visits to the families of our members, and was very useful in giving counsel, and in admonishing the erring ones, as well as in inviting those who felt desirous of investigating to attend our meetings and listen to the preaching of the Gospel. She was of a timid nature, and it was difficult for her to labor except in a social way or in family calls, but her labors in this sphere were abundantly useful to the infant church.

Gulielma's health was greatly broken by the nervous shock caused by the storming of Matamoros by the forces of Gen. Diaz, and among those consulted was an aged woman whose treatment in such cases had been useful to many. She bad long been a strict Romanist, and was quite profane and quarrelsome with her neighbors, and at 87 years of age we had no thought of her conversion. On one occasion when she called in the ministers of both missions were engaged in a weekly prayer meeting, and fearing that our exercises would disturb her, Angelita took her to the school room in order to entertain her until our prayer meeting should close. She began to ask Angelita the object of our gathering, and as she overheard the singing of a hymn was much pleased with it. Angelita invited her to attend our public meetings, which she promised to do. This was the first step which led to the conversion of Petra Garza de Mendez, the closing years of whose life were to show forth in a wondrous manner the power of the Gospel to redeem even those who might seem to be immovably fixed in the superstitious ideas which for more than fourscore years she had held as her hope of salvation.

A woman living near her home had a Bible and by invitation of this aged lady would go to read the Bible to her, and both were led by its influence to a full acceptance of the Protestant faith.

Not long after the occupation of the city by Gen. Escobedo a large body of his troops went in pursuit of Gen. Gonzalez, thus the troops for the defence of the city were reduced, and Gen. Cortina who had escaped from his detention as prisoner at the city of Mexico, had organized his followers and began to scour the plains and at times to attack the city.

One night as we were sitting in our room, occupied in our several tasks, my own being as usual that of translation, a sudden and terrific crash was heard, and in a moment we bounded to where we could have the protection of a double planking from the the balls which were coming in profusion and with stunning force. The first crash was however the only one which entered our building. An ounce ball had passed over our heads at an elevation of about two feet above them, when striking against a thick sheet of tin and just over the wire band at its edge, had bounded back into the middle of the floor, barely missing us in the rebound. The dread roar of one of the long field pieces made the enemy retire and the firing ceased.

Nearly every cloudy night or foggy morning these attacks were renewed, and as balls were falling all around our buildings we prepared a small room the sides of which were protected by benches, planking, bedding, and such useful books as presented a considerable surface to protect us from the stray balls. We had it thus barricaded to a height of about four feet from the floor, and so soon as we heard the discharge of musketry we went into this room and lying down upon the floor, were comparatively free from danger. Our Friend Agustin Gonzalez had prepared a pit, covered with strong beams and about a foot of earth, in which he could protect his family, and we had often thought of doing the same. The right of self defense by such means being licit and laudable.

Familiarity with danger had in a measure abated our fears, and by day when attacks were made, we scarcely gave them any attention whatever, and were often walking upon the streets, returning from a visit or some errand, some time after firing had begun. Several citizens had been wounded, one little girl of our acquaintance, whilst sleeping in her bed, had five teeth knocked out by a rifle ball, which left an ugly wound in each cheek, and one of our workmen had a ball pass through the head-board of his bed and through his pillow, but taking a downward course it fell to the floor. We would mathematically calculate these cases, and divide our population of 16,000 by that number and thus find that we stood comparatively little risk of injury.

Were we to admit that one peaceful citizen were wounded in each attack, we would still incur only one risk in 16,000, and were a ball to strike us the chances were more favorable to a slight injury than to a mortal wound, thus on the doctrine of probabilities we had a fair chance. But far above all was the thought that we were the children of a kind Heavenly Father, engaged in his service, and he had promised to be with such as placed their trust in him. Thus during seven months of close siege and frequent hostilities we were able quietly to go forward with our work with very few interruptions. The most heart-rending scene during the summer and fall was the burning of the ranches to the westward of the city, by order of Gen. Revueltas, then military commander of the city. The poor people were ejected from their dwellings and not allowed to save any of their valuables, whilst their buildings were burned before their eyes. In one case it was said that an infant was burned to death in the cradle, its mother being absent when their reed house, thatched with grass, was fired and in a few moments was reduced to ashes. This was a reprisal, or might be a victory, but it was to the poor victims, pillage and murder.

*A Victory*, alias *Pillage and Murder.*

# CHAPTER XIII.

Conversion of Luciano Mascorro. Incidents during
the siege. Death of Cástulo Salas during the
"big drunk" which followed the entry of the
forces of Gen. Cortina.

UP to this date our mission had no native evangelist, since the removal of Clemente A. Vivero,
and aside from the occasional exhortations of
Agustin Gonzalez and his more frequent exercises
of prayer, the native portion of the congregation took
no active part in the vocal exercises. We felt this to
be a great draw-back to our work, for native evangelists have much nearer access to the people, and
speak the language with greater ease. It is rare
indeed that a foreigner escapes some chronic peculiarity which marks him as a foreigner. The missionary
is no exception to this rule. Some peculiarity of
accent, some slight variation in the sound of a vowel,
some mistaken use of a verb, or a badly chosen
adjective, betray his foreign nationality.

We had long had a useful assistant in the press
room, but unexpected difficulties were paving the
way for his separation from our employ.

One afternoon as I was busy in the printing office
a young man handed me a letter which had been
given to him in another printing office in the city.
It was from a young man who had been connected
with the editorial work of a liberal paper in Mier,
and who had read "El Ramo de Olivo" as an exchange
paper, and desired to know more about the Society

87

of Friends which sustained such a paper. He had attended a few of the meetings of Clemente A. Vivero in that city, and had been an energetic member of a society of "Workmen" which had been organized there. He had also on one occasion delivered the public address in the plaza on the national celebration of the uprising at Dolores, the first stroke of Mexican Independence.

It was not an idle curiosity that prompted him to take this new step, and expose himself to the ridicule of his nearest relatives, and most intimate acquaintances. He was not only a decided liberal, but saw in Christianity as presented in "El Ramo de Olivo," something that could satisfy the longing of an immortal soul. He had lost all confidence in Romanism, and whilst in Mier in concert with his fellow compositors in the office of "La Lámpara" had issued for gratuitous circulation that cutting satire on Romish superstitions which has done more perhaps than any other pamphlet to open the eyes of the devotees of Rome to see the errors of that church, and the astonishing contrast between its pantomimes and the Gospel of Christ.

Completely weaned from Romanism, he had been living for some time with a brother who was a Mason, and had come under the excommunication issued by Bishop Montesdeoca against the members of that order. The Bishop had recently made his last visit to the towns along the Rio Grande above Matamoros, where he was met at every turn by criticisms from the public press and found but few sympathizers.

This interesting young man, since so well known wherever the Gospel has extended in Mexico, was simply invited to attend our next public meeting at the usual hour where he could best understand our work.

It was a night meeting, and the preaching was a simple exposition of the doctrine of repentance for the remission of sins. Luciano Mascorro, for such was his name, listened with attention, he was not only persuaded, but *felt* the power of the Gospel reaching his heart. He was henceforward a diligent attender and but a few weeks later applied for admission as a member, and was warmly welcomed by the brethren to a place in our midst.

The vacancy in our printing office was now filled and his rare typographical ability soon made a very decided improvement in the appearance of our publications.

The siege continued with unabated rigor, the mails were closed, and for a time it was necessary for all burials to take place in the costly cemetery inside the city walls. The three bridges across the ditch were taken up and the gateways filled in with piles of posts, whilst some wire fences were placed outside to prevent a sudden assault. Attacks were frequent, and on one occasion as Luciano was walking in the street a ball struck about two feet before him, imbedding itself in the earth. One afternoon as I was returning from Brownsville, which was our only outlet, coming around a bend on the street railway, where our car was in line with the east wall I could distinctly see from the car window the blaze of the two contending armies, as volley after volley was exchanged between the insurgents and the force of Ft. Iturbide, where the eastern wall reaches the river bank apposite Ft. Brown. I hastened home as I knew that they would be nearer in range and more exposed to danger than I was where I first saw the combat. On reaching home I found that Gulielma and Angelita had just returned from shopping on Commercial St. and had been walking in the streets during most of the combat. Such is the confidence inspired by continued exposure to danger, and familiarity with revolutions.

Notwithstanding these critical surroundings we decided to have the usual closing exercises of our school on Christmas night. Aside from the scholars several young people were to take part in the exercises, and a beautiful Christmas tree was arranged and filled with presents for the children, a special fund for this object having been raised by our members, amounting in that time of scarcity to some 16 dollars, most of which was spent in articles of clothing for the school children.

OPENING A BOX OF CHRISTMAS GIFTS.

The evening was fine, the house filled to overflowing, and no part of the exercises attracted more attention than the closing address to parents and children by Luciano Mascorro. It was his first public discourse in defense of the Gospel, and caused a

favorable impression on the audience, whilst the
elders of the church thought they saw there the plain
indication of a call to the ministry. He received the
most cordial counsels of the officers of the Society,
and soon after began to take part in the public exercises of our regular meetings. He had some months
previously been appointed Clerk of the Monthly
Meeting, held then as now at 8 P. M. of the first
Saturday of each month.

School opened again two weeks after New Years
and Angelita had been able to add quite a number of
children to the list, among others several grand-nieces
of Ramon Lozano, the Luther of Mexico. She had
been appointed as deaconess in November, 1876,
and each month she had to give an account of the
number of sick, and any other subject bearing on the
progress of the church, especially those things relating
to the female members. She was accordingly very
diligent in visiting the sick, and in counselling those
who had become careless in attending our meetings,
or had fallen into sinful habits. She was greatly
blessed in this labor for Christ, and received the most
cordial sympathy of the whole church, of which she
had become *servant*, as the Greek word implies.

As we have previously stated, our members had
nearly all refrained from taking any part in the
revolutionary struggle which placed Gen. Diaz in
the presidential chair. They were engaged in a more
important struggle, and amid the varying shades of
public opinion maintained a most strict neutrality.
One of our members had some time previously passed
over to Brownsville, where he had engaged in a small
grocery business, and was getting along well in trade.

He had a wife, some years younger than himself,
and a bright little boy was the father's joy and the
mother's pride. Prior to his union with our Society
he had been an intimate friend and partizan of Gen.

Cortina, who since his escape from prison in Mexico, had gathered his followers and besieged our city.

After the defeat of Gen. Diaz, at Hicamole, he had escaped in some way the vigilance of the forces at Tampico and by an unlooked for series of victories had taken possession of the national capital, although this event was unknown in Matamoros until 40 days after the flight of President Sebastian Lerdo de Tejada. Every other point had surrendered and a longer resistance here was useless. Yet Gen. Revueltas well knowing the character of Gen. Cortina, who after besieging us many months under various pretexts, had now declared in favor of Gen. Diaz, had determined not to permit his entry into the city. When Gen. Blanco was sent by Diaz to take command of the city, be determined to permit the peaceful entry of Gen. Cortina. The 19th of February was fixed upon, and flowers were strewn in the pathway of Cortina and his troops.

Cástulo Salas, the member of whom we have been speaking, determined to cross over the river above Matamoros, and accompany his old friend in the hour of triumph, and entered the city on horseback, but unarmed, in company with the army.

After the entry of Gen. Cortina a small bounty was distributed to the troops and they prepared for a big drunk, to celebrate their victory, not a few of the government troops getting more than half-seas-over in half a day. As the head-quarters of Gen. Cortina were opposite our printing office, then on Tenth St. corner of Bustamante, we returned home early in the afternoon as the drunken roughs were discharging firearms at random and thus endangering the lives of peaceful citizens. Early at night we closed our doors, for groups of drunken soldiers, mostly of Cortina's men were at the street corners near our house, still purchasing liquor and increasing the uproar. Just after dark we heard terrible shrieks at one of the grog shops, or rather a store with a bar on the front end of the counter, as is usual in groceries in Mexico, and then followed the shrill whistle of the police telling us that something had happened, yet we thought prudence the better part of valor, especially when dealing with drunkards, and kept our house closed until after day dawned the next morning.

Just after breakfast one of our members brought us a paper with the police report for the previous day, and we saw that Cástulo Salas had been struck down by the drunken crowd, one of his own party having struck him on the head with the breech of his gun, burying the lock in his brain.

A messenger soon called us to the bedside of the dying man, who was entirely unconscious, although he lingered most of that day. Gen. Cortina offered to bear the expense of the funeral, but the desires of his wife, and there being no proof of his being in any way culpable, induced us to take charge of the interment.

The following morning we attended the funeral, though quiet had not been restored in the streets, as a drunken officer fired six shots through the rear carriage as they went to the house, ready to take the friends of the deceased to the meeting, the carriage being empty at the time. We occupied the carriage on the return and it was with difficulty that we could induce the coachman to pass the same street corner, where he had previously been fired upon, though his aggressor had in the meanwhile been arrested, and was severely punished for his disorderly conduct.

This funeral was one of the most impressive I was ever permitted to attend, and never did I feel greater freedom and boldness to show how the mangled corpse of our brother warned us to avoid evil associations and yielding to temptation. The open doors were however crowded with roughs and quite a number of the associates of Cortina were seated in the room.

The 30th. of January had in previous years been kept as anniversary of the first organization of the Society, but owing to the state of public affairs it was decided to have as anniversary the last Sabbath of February, anniversary of the first meeting for worship opened by us in 1872, and which was kept in succeding years. This time a new platform, with Bible stand, and hand-rail had been arranged by some of our members who were carpenters and was placed in our meeting room that morning, giving it a much more inviting aspect.

Peace was once more restored to the nation, the prices of eatables which had risen considerably quickly fell to the usual rate, the mails were soon re-established, and our books which had been for the time limited to the city, began to be called for from distant points, whilst the attendance at our meetings began to increase and the work take a more inviting aspect.

Septentrional America. (Mexico.)

# CHAPTER XIV.

FTER the restoration of peace our members who had taken refuge in Brownsville began to return and thus our meetings began to increase in attendance, and early in the Spring the grand-nieces of Father Lozano who had been brought into our day school were admitted as members, and the eldest of these being earnest in her zeal for the progress of the Gospel, was one of a small band who met twice each week to practice singing and learn new hymns. The ability of Angela Aguilar was here displayed and many hearts were influenced in our public meetings by Gospel Truths taught in the sweet language of song. Luciano Mascorro was also an excellent singer and often in attendance at these gatherings, and once each week both the schools were brought together for one hour and trained in this useful exercise, and many truths sown in those young hearts may bear a rich harvest. I did not say tender hearts, for though many such there were, we had at that time in our school some pretty unruly children whose parents were friendly to our work, and but for their ungodly lives would have joined our Society. Protestantism had become popular and many who

95

had no use for the priests began extolling Protestantism, thinking it a free road to heaven. We had in our school the children of two noted bandits and highwaymen, one of whom had been shot as an outlaw, whilst the other was an officer in the army of Gen. Cortina, known better as the border ruffian *"El Tejon,"* (the badger,) a corpulent and daring fellow. He met me one day, praised our school, and said that he wanted to join our Society, as he admired the changed life of some of our members with whom he was acquainted. He reminded me of a man who was condemned to death in Greensboro, N. C. some years ago and whom I visited two days before his execution. Speaking of the visits of several of our ministers to his cell after his sentence, he said to me: "I have always leaned toward your Society," when stopping himself, he resumed, "No, I have always *leaned towards destruction*, but I always thought that you were right." This bandit could not help but realize that he was hastening toward destruction, but he was persuaded that Protestantism taught the way of life.

One morning just after school had opened his daughter was sent for in haste, with word that her father was dying. The circumstances of his death caused a deep impression on the class to which he belonged, and even *they* looked upon it as a direct judgment from God. He was intoxicated and drove along on horseback, and was just passing the house of a woman of bad character, and stopping his horse began speaking to her, when taking his revolver from his belt he fired at her. At the instant she held both hands aloft in surprise, when he discharged his pistol the ball passed through her hand, and striking the brick wall of the house, in the rebound struck him in the breast, and being imbedded near the heart caused death almost instantly. It was evidently no chance work, and Christian and infidel were alike awed by so unlooked for a termination of the life of "*El Tejon.*" How a ball should have struck so as to return like a boomerang, and with sufficient force to cause a mortal wound, and thus kill the one who fired it, is yet a mystery, but the fact itself was so evident that the Judge had no difficulty in declaring that it was a case of accidental suicide.

In May of that year we were called to the bedside of a dying woman in Brownsville, and as usual Angelita was one of the company. We had been sent for at a late hour the previous night, when it was not practicable to go as the ferry would not be open for us to return, and when we reached the house, next morning a Romish Priest was at her bedside. He had been sent for in the absence of the husband of the dying woman by some negresses who lived in the larger jacal in the same yard, and they claimed that the dying woman had solicited his coming, but she was evidently not conscious of what was passing around her. The first priest left to send the more daring superior of the order, who though known under another name are really Jesuit, and quite a controversy ensued in which Angelita boldly opened her Bible to answer the arguments of the priest, who was not a little surprised at her boldness. The husband of the dying woman assured the priest that both himself and wife were members of our meeting and that he had never heard her express a desire to confess, and was aware that she had sent for us the previous night. The group of Louisiana negroes however called the owners of the building who ordered our ejection in company with the husband on the ground that the latter paid no rent, and there being no remedy we stood in the yard, whilst the door was closed and the priest claimed that the woman confessed and received extreme unction, though in a few moments the door was opened to light the candles for she was dead.

By request of the husband we took charge of the
burial, and when we went to the house to take the
corpse to the Presbyterian Church the widowed husband was sitting by the fence, whilst his little ragged
girl, only two years old lay on a sheep skin under the
scorching sun by his side. She was weeping for her
mother, and had only partaken of some partly cooked
beans, and was really a most touching sight. We had
known them for several years, and were present at
their marriage, the father of this woman having been
a pillar in our church from the beginning, the first of
our converts in Mexico to join the throng which sur-
rounds the throne of God. We asked the father to
give us the little suffering child, which was brought
to our house that evening, and has ever since been
under our care, whom not a few of our friends will
remember having seen during our visit to our native
land in 1881.

The following day Gulielma, whose health was
still precarious, joined a company who went to bathe
in the Gulf, at Agua Dulce, and the weeping little
stranger spent the first week in her new home in the
arms of Angelita.

In August of the same year Gulielma went again
to the sea-side, and I was able to accompany her,
taking our adopted child with us, and leaving Angelita in charge of the school, and Luciano in charge
of the press work. It was during our absence that
Luciano first suggested to Angelita his offer of
marriage. It was not one of those lucifer matches, so
suddenly planned and executed, but a most deliberate
desire to further the cause of the Gospel of Christ,
so dear to each of them, and which was to be carried
out after the most mature and prayerful deliberation.
We were the first persons to be consulted by both
parties and were glad indeed that so appropriate a
union should open before them.

That summer was one of unusual prosperity in both the Missions at Matamoros and almost every month new members were added to our meeting, some from a decided preference to our tenets, others because they first received Christ through our ministry. One of the former class, father of a numerous family had been a very wicked man, but his conversion was real, and he became a pillar in the church.

The Mexican converts evince great independence of thought, carefully studying the Scriptures with desires to know the truth, and to receive it from Christ alone, and very unwilling that anything should hinder their doing the will of their Master. Casting aside the dogma of Papal infallibility, they rest less on the opinions of others than most Christians in a land where Romanism never held sway.

AZTEC EDUCATION.

Correcting a pupil with the pointed leaves of the Pita or Spanish Dagger. [Yucca gloriosa.]

The tongues signify reproofs. Aztec hieroglyphics always have eyes like a front view.

MEXICAN SCENERY, FALLS OF REGLA.

# CHAPTER XV.

PREPARATIONS FOR CHRISTMAS. RETURN OF THE FLORES FAMILY. REMARKABLE INSTANCE CONNECTED WITH THE ILLNESS AND DEATH OF PEDRO GONZALEZ. THE MARRIAGE OF ANGELITA.

AS the year 1877 was closing the school changed hands, for Angelita was arranging for her marriage and could not much longer retain her position. A family which had been very useful in aiding us to acquire language on our arrival, had afterwards returned to Monterey and from there to Lampazos, where the four daughters had charge of the public school for about two years. Returning to Camargo on the Rio Grande, they wrote to us offering to furnish us a teacher, and a month before Christmas Emilia Flores took charge of the school, and her three sisters assisted in the composing room and folding and stitching department, as our books had become numerous and the circulation over all Spanish America required greater activity in the publishing department.

A new era in the life of the church was inaugurated, the members were united and enthusiastic in their love for the work, a session of about thirty of the most earnest members met to arrange for the Christmas exercises of the two schools, who subscribed over twenty dollars for that object, and decided to have a regular tax list whereon every member could subscribe the amount he was willing to give monthly for the care of the poor and the requirements of church work.

101

The exercises were well arranged and the night being beautiful the hall was crowded to excess, the interior rooms of our dwelling were occupied by many of the mothers who having little babes were unwilling to pack in the crowd and who could see and hear through an open doorway, whilst all the windows were thronged and a crowd in all the doors opening to the street, where a policeman kept perfect order.

The exercises consisted mainly of declamations in both prose and poetry by the children, and that night hundreds heard for the first time of the love of Jesus and the greatness of his mission through their instrumentality. Brief discourses from several of our leading members opened and closed the exercises, and thus a favorable impression was made upon many who had been led to attend from a mere idle curiosity to see the Protestants.

One of the most interesting incidents of the winter was the death of Pedro Gonzalez, who though not a member had long read our publications with interest, and now that he neared his close he often sent for us, and many interesting seasons were enjoyed as we read the Scriptures and sung hymns by his bedside, and were engaged in exhorting him to confidence in the sacrifice of Christ, and some of our company knelt in prayer with him.

His wife was a strict Romanist, and a considerable part of one side of the room was occupied by an altar crowned with pictures and images of Saints, to whom she often burned wax candles. Her husband declared that he had no confidence in these figures, but rested plainly on the sweet words of his loving Savior. His wife sent for a priest one day, but as the dying man expressed his conviction that their teachings were wrong, the priest left quite abruptly. As some tried to circulate word that he had retracted, his wife had the kindness to send us a letter stating that our visits had been a source of great comfort to her husband and that he died, as he had lived, a Protestant.

I must not omit to mention our first acquaintance with this person and the permanent fruit which grew out of it. In one room of his house was a cigarette factory with five operatives, and the old gentleman was usually to be seen sitting in the doorway. On one occasion as M. M. Binford was passing along distributing tracts he accosted Pedro and offered him one. A conversation ensued and Micajah was invited to enter, and gave tracts to all the workmen but one. This one was son-in-law of Pedro, and was so fearful of being contaminated with heresy that he dared not even look up to see the heretic. The tracts were read and commented upon, and on the next visit this young man secretly wished for a tract but did not dare to ask for it. Soon after this young man began attending our meetings, and is now one of our most successful evangelists, and endued with a large share of spiritual discernment. His name is Francisco Peña. His labors however do not enter until near the close of the present volume.

It was not until March of 1878 that Angela Aguilar was united in marriage with Luciano Mascorro. Few countries take greater care in regard to marriage than Mexico, and the laws render clandestine marriages impossible. The parties go before the civil judge with two male witnesses for each party, all of whom must be persons of known good character and residents of the town where the marriage is to take place. The name and consent of parents, and the names of the grand-parents, as well as the place of residence of all these ancestors is carefully noted down, and the whole written out in a formal declaration, three copies of which are posted on the doors of at least three of the offices of the city council and judges. The names also usually appear in the public newspapers during the two weeks which intervene

between the first and second presentation before the
judge. When one of the parties has recently arrived
from some other point the proceedings are delayed
until the authorities of the place in which he or
she formerly resided can be duly consulted as to their
clearness of like engagements there. In case one of
the parties is a widow or widower a certificate of the
civil register of deaths and interments from the place
where said party deceased is indispensable, and thus
it is not unusual for two months to elapse between
the first and second presentation before the civil
magistrate. On the second- presentation, if no obstacle has presented, the judge reads the report of the
first presentation and asks the parties, who remain
seated, usually side by side, though this is not necessary, if it is still their free and voluntary desire to
take each other in marriage, and on receiving an
affirmative answer from each party, he proceeds to
read the duties and obligations of married life in a
legal point of view, a document as ably written as
any I have ever seen upon marriage.

In Mexican law marriage is a union for life, no
divorce being granted, and though a temporary
separation may be legally arranged in case of adultery,
yet even then neither party is free to contract matrimony, and the law hopes even in these cases for an
ultimate reconciliation and reunion of the parties.

This law is based upon the Roman Catholic inter-
pretation of the words of Christ:— "Whosoever shall
put away his wife, saving for the cause of fornication,
*causeth her to commit adultery:*" arguing that having
already committed adultery was the cause of our
Savior's exception to such an act causing her to
commit adultery, although in Mat. xix. 9. the words
of Christ do not admit this evasion. However it
is very evident that the people of Mexico, and indeed
of Spanish America in general are not prepared to
admit divorce laws, nor are the results of these laws

in other countries sufficiently encouraging to convince them that they are desirable.

On the other hand as their law limits all accusation of adultery to the injured party, though having no legal sanction, concubinage is not uncommon among the wealthy, particularly foreign merchants, mostly French, Spanish and Italian, who live with women without legal marriage. As the Romish Priests view the liberal government as their enemy, usurper of their temporal power, when parties present themselves before them for marriage, they are not asked whether they have contracted marriage before the judge or not, but are united in matrimony by the church, though one or both may be already married by law. This causes the most lamentable results, as many unprincipled young men marry before the priest, and after a while, finding another bride more to their taste forsake their church wife and marry the new one before the civil judge. The church may excommunicate the bridegroom, but the deserted wife has no redress, her children are illegitimate in a legal point of view, and can receive but a limited part of their father's property.

The legal side is not so tolerant, for when a man leaves his legal wife and marries another in the church, he can at her accusation be punished for adultery, and her children are his legal heirs, and no man can leave by will more than one fifth of his property, except to his heirs at law, so that this class of marriages is rare. One took place some years ago in Soto la Marina, but the priest who had counselled and solemnized the marriage was imprisoned as abettor of immorality, and only released on the payment of a heavy fine.

Recently some of the authorities, especially the Governor of Coahuila have forbidden the priests to marry parties except in view of a certificate from the civil magistrate, or baptize any children not registered on the civil register. Over 700 children were registered in one month in the city of Saltillo alone in execution of this law, and the Bishop became so incensed that he forbade the priests administering the sacraments, as they call them, until the law be repealed. Bishop Montesdeoca who issued this order is famous as one of the clerical embassy which went to Miramar to offer their government to a foreign potentate, and he held the Gospels whilst Maximilian took the oath of office as emperor of Mexico. Archbishop Labastida (who was regent of that imported monarchy, sustained by the troops of Napoleon III.) does not seem to approve of the course of Montesdeoca, fearing it may lead to the expulsion of the priests, as the government expelled the sisters of Charity in 1875, for like infractions of the Reform Laws established by President Juarez.

The civil power does not prohibit but rather encourages the parties to ratify their marriages before their respective churches, and if the marriage takes place at the house of the parents of the bride, or any private residence, the religious ceremony may take place immediately after the civil marriage, and some times judge and priest are both present during the whole ceremony.

The Protestant churches uniformly require that the parties present proof by their witnesses of having complied with the law, the solemnization taking place immediately after the civil marriage has been performed. Thus Luciano and Angelita, accompanied by their witnesses, arrived from the office of the civil magistrate and entered the meeting already gathered for the occasion and took their seats at a table fronting the preacher's desk, with their waiters seated at either side, after a discourse on the religious aspect of marriage they arose to ratify before the assembled church that act which had just been sanctioned before the legal authority.

It was a beautiful night, the hall was adorned with vases of flowers, and the seats were crowded, the windows and doors also closely packed with spectators, the presence of a policeman preserving order without difficulty. The supper was prepared in a large interior room, those who had been invited passed out following the couple to the seats at the table, the audience dispersing so quietly that the policeman, who was a member of our meeting, was invited to a seat at the table, where the blessing of God on the social gathering was again invoked and a sweet solemnity pervaded the happy festive occasion.

AZTEC PRIEST SACRIFICING HUMAN HEARTS TO HUITZILOPOCHTLI.

# CHAPTER XVI.

CONVERSION OF JULIO GONZALEZ GEA. RECOGNITION
OF LUCIANO MASCORRO AS MINISTER OF THE GOS-
PEL. VISIT TO SAN FERNANDO. EPIDEMIC FEVER. THE
ADMISSION OF I. BOLADO. CHRISTMAS EXERCISES.

ABOUT a month after the marriage, as we were
about sitting down to tea a very pleasant man in
middle life stepped up and introduced himself by
showing us a note written on a blank leaf in his
diary and signed by Clemente A. Vivero. He stated
that whilst passing through Reynosa he had met on
the bank of the river a very strangely clad fisherman,
who had told him about our work in Matamoros, and
whose clear declaration of the Gospel was very much
in accord with his own convictions. He had served in
the war against the North Americans in 1847, and
was severely wounded in the bombardment of Vera
Cruz, by a shell from the fleet of Gen. Scott. He was
then a mere lad, and like many others endeavored to
defend his native city from an unjust foreign invasion.

During the French invasion he had taken no part,
as he had near relatives in both contending armies,
whose blood he was unwilling to shed. He had however recently occupied a position in the government
of the State of Chihuahua, and having four children
was very desirous to direct them aright in religious
matters. His name was Julio Gonzalez Gea.

He began attending our meetings regularly and two
months later he was admitted a member as were also
his children at his request.

109

He took great interest in our meetings and his children began attending our school, except his eldest daughter who was his house-keeper. As he lived near the central square, in his profession of watch repairer, his children had to come quite a distance and were often treated with abusive language and brick-bats by the boys going to the public schools. This was to them quite a trial, and the more so as they were near relatives of Col. Cristo former military commander of the government forces stationed in Matamoros.

Julio Gonzalez Gea was soon after appointed Secretary of our monthly business meeting, and thus was present at the public recognition of Luciano Mascorro as Minister of the Gospel in the Society of Friends. The Foreign Mission Committee of Indiana Yearly Meeting had given its sanction, and in part had suggested the plan of the meeting. The monthly meeting was on the night preceding the public recognition, which took place at the close of our public meeting for worship in the afternoon of September 12th, 1879.

During this meeting Luciano was seated with the elders and deacon in a row in front of the audience and facing the platform where the secretary, who was to read the minute of the meeting was seated at my side for the first time.

The meeting opened as usual with reverent prayer to God to accompany this solemn occasion with a special blessing, and the singing of hymns of praise to him for past favors and blessings. This was followed by a discourse on the origin, nature and obligations of the Gospel ministry, setting forth that they are in no wise priests or successors of those who sacrificed at the altar, but successors of the prophets who were specially called to ~~called to~~ teach the people the will of God. This call was the first great requisite of a Christian minister, when he should consecrate all his natural and acquired abilities to the full discharge of his duty in order to insure success in the work.

The sermon was listened to with the most marked attention, and is the only one which at the request of several of our members was embodied in a pamphlet which was published in order to show the wide difference between the Romish priesthood sacrificing at the altar, and the Christian ministry boldly and clearly expounding the will of God, opening to their hearers the pages of his holy word as recorded for our instruction in righteousness.

After the sermon I took him by the hand in the name of the Foreign Mission Committee, extending to him their cordial fellowship in the ministry of the Gospel. Each of the elders as well as the deacon followed, the secretary closing the series of personal exhortations and recommendations to the care and guidance of the great Head of the church. After the meeting was dismissed quite a number of members followed with similar exhortations, which always accompany the appointment of church officers as a natural expression of that earnest zeal which characterizes the Mexican converts to evangelical Christianity.

Soon after this event Luciano paid a visit to San Fernando, and although great alarm had already existed in Matamoros about yellow fever, in no place was its approach less looked for than from the quiet little village of San Fernando, situated on a limestone bluff on the banks of a beautiful river flowing over a rocky bed. Thus when Luciano left for that village little did we think of the danger to which he was exposing himself. The fact that a fever of a very fatal nature had unfolded itself in San Fernando became known to us a few days after he left us, for as there was no resident physician the people had sent 120 miles for one of our city physicians. When Luciano reached there he found every house full of sick people, the village proper having 2000 inhabitants had about 300 sick and the death rate was so

alarming that quite a number fled to our city, eight
of whom came down with the disease, which the
Mexican physicians declared to be yellow fever, in a
few days. Luciano found but little chance for Gospel
labor and hastily returned and was prostrated by the
disease a few days after reaching home. He had
contracted the disease in San Fernando, and as was
the case with the other refugees did not communicate
the disease to others. Yellow fever does not appear
to be contagious, but gradually extends from place
to place either by a slow land travel, or may be taken
in the holds of ships or in closed packs of goods.
Those who are accustomed to it can readily tell it on
entering the room, owing to a peculiar odor arising
from the patient. There may have been a few spora-
dic cases originated in the city, and although we had
steamers touching at Bagdad, our offing 30 miles from
the city, it was not imported by sea.

Soon after his recovery, on one occasion as our
usual night meeting was drawing to a close a man
expressed a desire to become a member of our Society,
and I was surprised when I learned that he lived at
Jimenez, about 180 miles south of Matamoros. He
had however several times attended our meetings
when in this city. He was a near relative of the only
family of our members who possessed even a moder-
ate share of worldly goods, and was himself owner of
considerable landed property besides his residence in
that village, and a house and lot in this city adjoining
the lot purchased for our meeting house. He seemed
truly converted and zealous in the cause, and has
labored hard to extend the knowledge of Christ
among his fellow townsmen. This was the first case
of receiving a non-resident member to our meeting,
but he has been quite useful in the work, and is a
stable Christian. Our Christmas exercises that year
were well arranged, the valedictory in verse delivered by María Gonzalez y Cilicea, daughter of our

Friend Julio Gonzalez Gea, who took an active part in all our gatherings and aided greatly in stimulating the work. Thus God was gradually preparing new laborers for the extension of the work of Christ in Mexico.

.rza House, Palenque, Prior to the Conquest.

A WAYSIDE RANCH, OR COUNTRY RESIDENCE.

# CHAPTER XVII.

JOURNEY TO GÓMEZ FARÍAS. THE WORK AT MATA-
MOROS. BIRTH OF S. P. MASCORRO. REMOVAL TO
SAN FERNANDO. RETURN AND ILLNESS OF ANGELI-
TA. DEATH OF THEIR CHILD.

THE winter was an interesting time in our mission,
as it was characterized by events which to a
certain extent exercised a notable influence on
the whole work. Early in January as I was busy
in the press room B...... S...... of San Fernando
entered, and told me that I could have a seat in his
carriage as far as that village.

He was desirous that I should go to Gómez Farías
and see his uncle, Father Lozano, whose movement
was undeniably the first effort to introduce a religious
reformation into Mexico. I accepted his offer and we
started the same evening.

As illustrating missionary journeys in Mexico, and
to give an inside view of the character of the villagers I shall venture to delay the reader to accompany
me in the imagination in my wanderings. We left
Matamoros at 4. P. M. on the 14th, of January 1879.
I will give the following extracts from my Diary.

"Jan. 14th. We reached a paraje, or camping-ground, in 'El
Llano de las Guerras,' near the outlet known as 'El Moquete,' to
which a channel had been cut to drain the lagoon south of Mata-

moros. We slept in the carriage, and the *mozos* sent with us by the owner of the carriage slept on the ground. The night was cold, but I had brought an extra large shawl and blanket for sleeping out when necessary, as in winter we feel the cold as much as the natives. Next morning, the 15th, we crossed 'El Moquete,' and proceeded, without any incident of importance, to another camping-ground, known as 'El Llano de las Mugeres,' where another large freight train of ox-carts camped soon after we did, the leader of which was a well-known *bracado.* We started at half-past three o'clock the next morning, so as to let our mules graze on a grassy plain by a pond of water. We made coffee as usual, and were soon crossing the immense grassy plain known as 'Llano del Tejon.' A herd of prong-horn antelopes gazed at us in wonder and finally went skipping off over the plain. Nothing of importance called our notice until noon, when we reached this village, there being much uniformity in the scenery, and no noise except the nightly howls of the packs of prairie wolves in the thickets.

"We were warmly received by old acquaintances. I did not find Prudencio Reyna at home, but was welcomed by his children.

"17th. Walked down to the river before breakfast, and after breakfast went out to the cemetery, which is full of new graves, victims of the late pestilence. Most of the females of the village are dressed in black for near relatives who have died during the epidemic. The cemetery is surrounded by a high limestone wall, sustained by buttresses, which are covered by stone crosses. There are many arched vaults built on the outside of the wall, but opening on the inside. The entrance doorway is adorned with pillars and elaborate designs, with an urn over each pillar, and a large central stone cross. Over the doorway is the following Latin inscription:

'PULVUS ES ET IN PULVEREM REVERTERES.

Á PRESB. R. LOZANO ANNO MDCCCL.'

"This is a reminiscence of the evangelical priest, to whose liberal views is due much of the progress of the Gospel in this portion of Mexico.

"In the view of that doorway, the iron grating giving me a view of scores of new graves, I opened the book written by R. Lozano and read these words: 'The goodness and mercy of God shine forth in all his words. *Death* is not a wrathful vengeance of God, but a law of nature, as is also *life.* If in this world that man alone is happy who is disposed to forgive injuries, God can not be so in heaven with eternal hatred to mankind, and when on earth he gave his life for all mankind and prayed for his enemies; it is therefore, a real impiety, a positive insult, and a great outrage to his goodness, to believe that all is wrath, vengeance and punishment to man. God had made of our life a *proof,* not a punishment, and this proof consists in the combat between good and evil passions, between matter and spirit, and only thus was it possible to place the liberty of man and let him choose between good and evil.'

"It was natural to reflect, where are those who have so recently left this world, and what will their future be? I looked in the book before me and find that not a word has Lozano given about the resurrection and final judgment, except in the language of the Bible. He quotes Matthew xxv; Mark xiii; Luke xxi; John v; Acts xvii, and Corinthians xv; also II Thessalonians ii; closing with the words of Paul in Romans xiv: 'If Christ died and rose again, it is because he is to be judge of the living and of the dead.' Like our early friend, Daniel Phillips, in his 'Proteus Redivivus,' he seemed to think best to state Scripture truths in Scripture language.

After giving two quarto pages of texts in regard to the final judgment, and eternal rewards and punishments, he ventures the following expressions about eternal fire: 'This devouring fire, unextinguishable fire, eternal fire, outer darkness, this place of reprobates, this gnashing of teeth, which is spoken of in the preceding texts, is what the Evangelical priest and Mexican Church understand by hell—damnation and eternal fire, believing that is equivalent to a perpetual separation from the grace and friendship of God, and the continual remorse caused by said separation.'

"In the evening I visited the town hall, and was introduced to the various authorities of the village. On returning to the Market, I met Marcos Galindo, and had considerable conversation with him in regard to the plan of salvation through Christ; several others standing by listened with interest. He purchased some books in our office a few weeks ago, and seems sincerely desirous to know what true Christianity is.

"18th. Cold and damp, so I could not venture out much until evening, when I went to see Prudencio Reyna, and had a most interesting time with his family. Later a soldier, who had called on me in the morning returned and asked for some books. He had a Bible, and was acquainted with A. J. Parks, former missionary at Cadereita, to whose preaching he has listened. Through him the tracts were read by quite a number of the soldiers. Afterwards I answered a number of questions from inquiring persons, and had ample oportunity to declare the gospel to about a dozen who were present.

"19th. Sabbath morning, I arose with earnest prayer to God to bless the labors of the day. Walked out for solemn waiting upon him for guidance. On returning Marcos Galindo came to see me, and we talked together for over an hour about the plan of salvation and the divine offices of Jesus Christ. He gave his own experience, and seems truly converted to God. He looked over our disciplinary rules and took a copy with him; he seems ready to renounce Rome and accept the Gospel even in the face of persecution. One of the by-standers was convinced that these teachings were true, and after Marcos left, another came up and listened to a more extended conversation with this latter person, so that the forenoon was full of rich blessings from on high.

"At the dinner table several questions were asked, and an extended exposition of our work was given in the presence of the whole family. I then went to the river to take the sunny air, and on returning, a soldier who has been attending Protestant worship in Mexico had called for some books. After some conversation, I gave him a hymn book, and then went to see Prudencio Reyna, where I had a very edifying time with his family. Returning to supper, the soldier brought one of his companions to see me, and after leaving this latter returned with another companion, bought a Bible, and accepted several tracts. The soldier who came first now returned, and received a Testament, which I loaned to him, and gave him some copies of 'El Ramo de Olivo.' The owner of a neighboring ranch came to get books for a school on his ranch, and received several evangelical tracts. Thus closed a day of most constant opportunity to invite wanderers to Christ, the only hope of salvation.

"20th. This morning I have been very busy writting letters and getting passports for some things I am sending to Matamoros, and arranging to start to-morrow for Jimenez. I learn that some effort has been made to try to hinder our opening a place of worship here by some bigoted Romanists, who have influence with the authorities.

"Before bidding farewell to San Fernando, in my outward journey, I must not omit two visits made to the house of my kind host, and both partially on my account, and both from influential women of the town; one from Adelaida—de Lozano, wife of the second magistrate of the Supreme Court, was a pleasant one. She brought with her two orphan children they have adopted, and was very sociable, and evidently of a pious disposition. I was informed that when in Victoria, with her husband, she attended mass a few times, but said to several intimate friends that the treasure she most prized in religious matters is a New Testament she has for her constant use at home. She received me kindly, and talked freely upon all social and religious topics.

"The other visit was as opposite as could be well imagined. The work of the few days I had spent there, and the warm welcome giving me by several influential residents, had not failed to alarm the extreme Roman element, whose chief representative there was a French lady, teacher of the girls' school, who, in violation of the laws, was teaching 'Ripalda's Catechism' and 'French Elements' in the public primary school. Supposing that I intended at once arranging for permanent mission work, she came around to see my host, to expostulate with him for bringing to town a *heretic,* more to be dreaded than the yellow fever, whose victims filled the cemetery.

"I had been told that neither Spanish nor French females can extemporize discourse but, I confess that I never heard a more energetic difcourse from a female orator in my native land."

The results were soon apparent for my host was ordered out of his house for having brought a heretic to town, and even when the owners were assured that I was to leave on the following morning he was only permitted to remain in the house by paying double the former rate of rent.

The following description of a night by the way-side may serve to illustrate the pleasures of camping out in Mexico.

"The lofty peaks of the Sierra Madre, rising far above the rough summits of the Sierra de San Cárlos, lent a bold and pleasing aspect to the western horizon. The ground was everywhere rough and rocky, and our horses began to weary as we reached the table-land, and could see the loftier trees which rose in the distance, denoting the site of a large stock ranch called 'El Encinal,' which we reached just before dark. * * * * Our saddle blankets of Sisal grass were spread upon the ground, and as I had brought shawls and a flannel blanket, I rested quite comfortably, and being weary with a ride of 54 miles, and unaccustomed to the saddle, I slept very soon after dark. I awoke at 3 A. M. and my guide being chilly, built a fire, whilst I walked away from the firelight to take a view of the starry heavens: We were in the centre of a vast table-land fully 1000 feet above the sea level; which gave us a better field for observation than I had anticipated, and not a cloud interrupted the view of the calm starlight of the southern heavens. Every thought of fatigue was lost in a moment as, resting its base on the plain the southern cross stood bold and brilliant before me. I seemed to imbibe for a moment that enthusiasm which must have filled the heart of Vasco de Gama, and his companions, as their eyes rested for the first time upon so bright a model of what they held in such high veneration. Other groups of stars, which I now beheld for the first time, revealed to me what I had so long desired to see, the brightest gems of the southern heavens. I had never in my previous visits to the Tropic of Cancer been able to see, and perhaps I should not on this occasion had I not slept upon the ground. The perpendicular position of the Cross at the time I first saw it was the most favorable that could be desired, and my pious guide called my attention to it with a feeling bordering on adoration."

Passing onward through Jimenez, where I found some who had been readers of "El Ramo de Olivo," and thence to the Ranch of San Matias, residence of our Friend Ignacio Bolado, whose wife was still a Roman Catholic although she received us kindly and seemed willing to listen to the religious conversations which I had with her husband, the first step toward her conversion, which took place about two years afterwards.

Ignacio very kindly secured me a guide and loaned me a horse and saddle, and from thence I crossed the Tamaulipa Oriental, at times passing one or two days without seeing human habitations, when I entered the more tropical region which was clearly noticeable on reaching Llera.

The road which we had traversed since leaving Jimenez was through a region abounding in jaguars and pumas, as well as the ocelot, or leopard cat, and the tiger cat. The puma is very destructive to herds, being especially fond of colts. The parrots abound wherever there are streamlets.

We were kindly entertained at Llera by Pragedis Balboa, a very liberal minded man who conversed very freely on religious matters and who has ever been kind to our missionaries when passing through the village.

Passing onward from Llera we began ascending the Sierra Madre chain amid a well-watered but precipitous region, and had to descend the mountains by zigzag paths, so steep that I dared not traverse them on horseback.

After sleeping all night among the clouds on one of the elevated table lands, we descended to a river valley where giant thorny reeds made our pathway perilous. Soon after crossing the stream over a rough bed of loose stones as large as pumpkins, we entered a dense tropical forest where giant trees bound together with vines and filled with parrots and other tropical birds formed a rough and picturesque passage between grotesque and precipitous mountains with projecting rocky ledges on either hand of the narrow valley, which led us after a journey of about seven miles from the ford, to the beautiful tropical village of Gómez Farías. Here we hoped to find one of our members whose wife was also an attender of our meetings, and who had recently removed here from Matamoros. We hoped to be refreshed by their company ere going to visit Father Lozano, which had been the principal object of my visit to this remote mountain village.*

Pablo Ibarra was of native origin and his wife had been born in this village. He had joined our Society whilst residing in Matamoros, where he was occupied as a water carrier. He had returned to this village and was servant of the presiding officer of the town, and it seems that like the little captive girl in the house of Naaman the Syrian, he had told his master so much about our work that he was desirous of seeing me, and was ready to do all in his power to enable me to gain access to the people.

Another object of my journey was to learn the fate of our colporteur who had left Matamoros some months previously and who was last heard from at Victoria, but had gone forward in the direction of Tula and Santa Bárbara, and who we feared might have either suffered at the hands of his enemies or have succumbed to disease. He had accompanied Luciano Mascorro on his visit to San Fernando and had thus been exposed to the epidemic fever which had spread alarm in all parts of Tamaulipas. I had intended to go forward as far as Antiguo Morelos in search of him, as he formerly resided there.

The wild beauty of the tropical forest was not more agreeable than the the scenery where the hand of man had subdued nature, and banana orchards. coffee trees and pine-apple gardens greeted the eye.

"I began inquiring for our friend Pablo Ibarra, and on reaching the door his wife ran out to receive me, overjoyed at so unexpected a visit. I supposed that her husband was inside, and entered hastily to salute him, but what was my surprise as on turning around the door I saw our colporteur, Calixto Lara, with a large supply of books and tracts. After a genuine Spanish hug I asked him how he knew that I was coming, to which he replied that he had not even thought such an event possible. Impressed with a belief that in this village he would be able to sell books enough to pay $2, which he was owing in Santa Bárbara for his horse; and that he would even have an opportunity to preach to the people, he had left the latter village two days before, and but for my late start from Llera, both of us would have reached the same house at the same hour for the same purpose. He was putting on his coat to go and see Father Lozano, but we must now wait for dinner. A boy ran hastily to the sugar mill to call Don Pablo, who was as overjoyed as any of us. Whilst dinner was preparing his wife spoke to him in a low whisper, and he grasped his cleaving knife and started out ·the back door, returning in a few moments with a large cluster of bananas."

"After dinner Pablo went with us to the ranch known as 'La Chinaca,' residence of Father Lozano, about a mile and a half from town. The descent was rough, and when it rains is very slippery.

"After passing through a field of sugarcane we came in sight of the house, a long reed structure with a palm leaf roof, as are all the houses in Gómez Farías. Father Lozano was dressed in the usual style of a city lawyer, his clothes the worse for the wear, probably those he wore when *mentor* of the State Congress as our legislature is called. He received us with warm-hearted kindness and Christian affability. He is extremely sociable, humble in his assertions, and charitable even to his enemies. He has the true spirit of nature's nobleman, as some one has called the agricultor, and says that food raised by the sweat of the brow is much sweeter than when purchased with money."

"February 2d, 1879. This was the most remarkable day in my missionary labor in this land. The morning was slightly uncomfortable, but as soon as breakfast was served our colporteur and Pablo Ibarra were passing about town arranging for a public meeting. The only place well seated was the old Catholic Mission Chapel, now used for the public school, and permission was readily granted for its use. At 3 P. M. a company of about 160 persons, including nearly all the principal residents, and a fair proportion of females had gathered in the chapel. Calixto Lara briefly stated the object of our mission. I followed in prayer, and then read some verses of John IV: following with an exposition of the same. The audience was greatly moved by the clear and simple teaching of the Gospel, so that very many shed tears and came forward at the close to express their satisfaction with our visit to their village."

Ere I returned to Matamoros, Angelita had given birth to a son, whom they had named Samuel Purdie Mascorro, and of whose future service in the cause of Christ the joyful parents entertained fond hopes. A month later they removed to San Fernando, hoping to open mission work there, but met with the most decided opposition. On writing a petition to the Mayor to register a place of worship, Luciano was fined $20, for not using stamped paper, a requisite of which he was ignorant, and this proceeding was without precedent and probably illegal. Against the will of an ignorant and obstinate Mayor there was no immediate remedy, their object was to have him imprisoned for inability to pay the fine, and they boasted that they would have him sweep the streets. Two of his acquaintances paid the fine, but no attention was given to the subject when brought again before the Council, and even the recommendation of the Commanding General at Matamoros, brother of the Mayor, was useless in trying to get this officer to permit the opening of Protestant worship there.

These were severe trials to the young mother, who feared the consequences of her husband's arrest. On regaining his liberty he came to Matamoros to try an appeal to the Governor, and as Angelita was suffering from pain in the breast, she came to get medical advice. The severity of the journey aggravated her disease, and when she reached our house she was removed from the carriage to a bed where she lay for some weeks in the most intense suffering. All hope of her recovery seemed to vanish several times, and it was not until the 10th of June, that she was able to sit up a part of the time. It had been necessary to wean the child, which was a severe stroke to it and on the day Angelita arose from the bed it was attacked with brain fever and after lingering a few days it died.

This was a severe blow to the young parents but was met with Christian resignation.

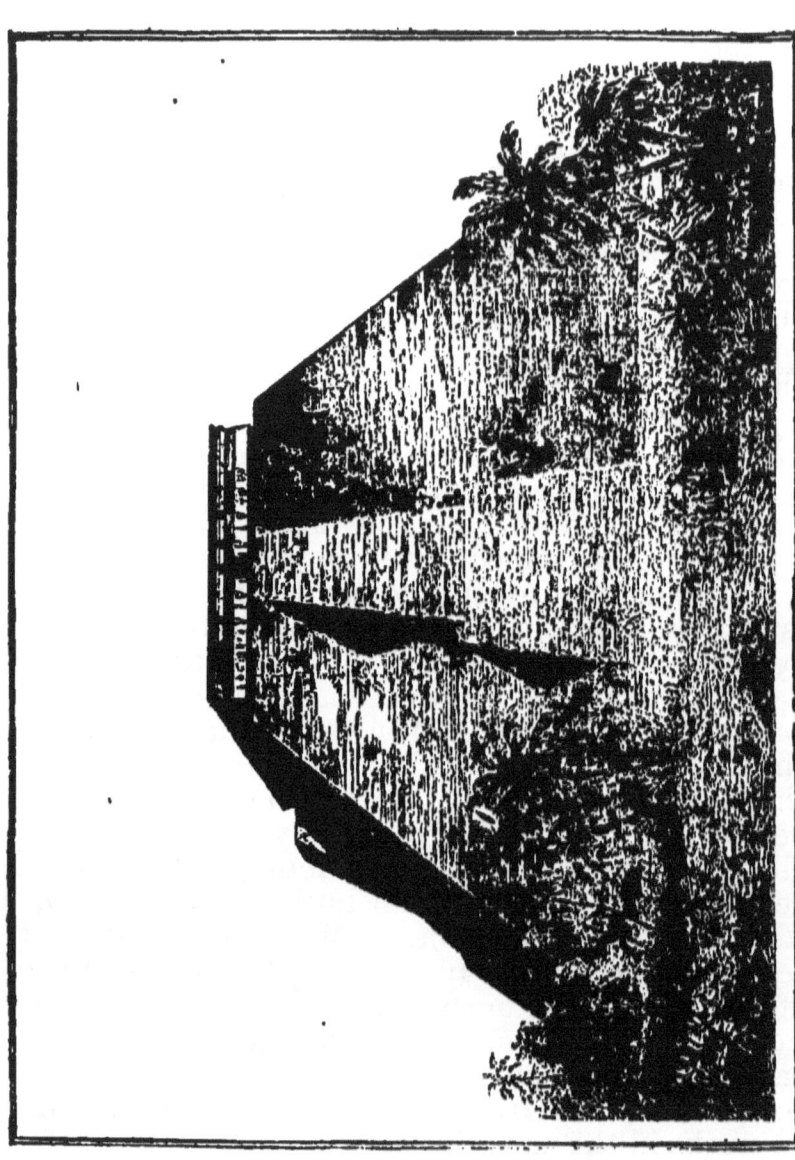

GREAT PYRAMID OF UXMAL, YUCATAN.

# CHAPTER XVIII.

INTEREST IN THE GOSPEL AT FARÍAS. MISSIONARY JOURNEY OF LUCIANO MASCORRO THROUGH TAMAU-LIPAS. RETURN IN COMPANY WITH CALIXTO LARA. HINDRANCES TO THE PERMANENT OCCUPATION OF GÓMEZ FARÍAS. APPEAL FROM YUCATAN.

FTER my return from Gómez Farías a few months elapsed before any news was received from that point as to the feeling of the people toward the Gospel work. Copies of "El Ramo de Olivo" were sent to several of those who had attended the meeting held there during my visit and these leaflets were fanning into a flame the desire to hear the preaching of the Gospel manifested by those villagers. The distance however seemed for a time to hinder any effort to establish a mission there, and had we received no further solicitations we might have desisted from further efforts.

A few months after my arrival at home I received a letter from the teacher of the public school, Francisco Zamora, requesting further information about our religious tenets and manifesting a desire to help in the work. This resulted in further correspondence and it was deemed prudent for Luciano to traverse the whole state and determine at what point it would seem desirable to locate a permanent work.

At that time, with the exception of Tampico, no point south of Matamoros had a resident missionary, and it was a matter of great importance to attempt a wider distribution of the evangelical laborers, and this visit was largely beneficial in this direction.

He left Matamoros on horseback and alone, and on the second night of his journey met a company whose leader seemed to take an interest in the Gospel and to whom he preached the word, and having supplied them with tracts pursued his journey. This interview by the wayside led to the conversion of a whole family at a ranch called El Encinal, and where a Presbyterian missionary preaches regularly, though the people would have preferred to have us organize the work there. This man has named one of his sons Esteban Grellet Garcia, in honor of Stephen Grellet the French Quaker evangelist.

Luciano stopped a few days in San Fernando and then pursued his journey, stopping for evangelical labor at El Encinal, where he was hospitably entertained by his wayside convert, and thence to Jimenez where he was instrumental in strengthening the faith of Ignacio Bolado, and in removing in some measure the prejudices which his wife had imbibed against the Protestant religion.

Pursuing his journey he found some access to the people at Padilla and Güemez and delayed a week at Victoria, in order to ascertain what openings there might be for mission work in that city, and then hastened forward to Gómez Farías, entering through the same gorgeous scenery of the Peñon pass, which I had entered nine months previously.

He found the people rejoiced at his arrival, and in Francisco Zamora he found an earnest convert and a ready coadjutor, whilst many of those who had listened to me, gladly met to hear him.

Luciano remained five weeks in this beautiful mountain village, being joined providentially by our colporteur Calixto Lara. Meetings were held twice each week and the quiet influence of social religious labor was very beneficial in establishing the converts. After this tarriance, news of revolutionary movements led them to return hastily to Matamoros, where they arrived about the end of October.

One Sabbath evening as the assembled worshippers were gathered at religious service at 49 Calle de Bravo, Luciano and Calixto entered unexpectedly, and the former gave a detailed narrative of his religious labors during an absence of nearly three months.

About this time an urgent appeal was received from Mérida in Yucatan, requesting us to establish a mission in that peninsula, and whilst the opening among such a dense population might seem especially desirable, and all the more so because the appeal was entirely unsolicited, and the firm belief of the solicitors that a Friends' Mission was particularly adapted to their needs, yet the crowd of work attendant upon building a place of worship in Matamoros, and the continued ill health of Angelita seemed to prevent our accepting for the time being the vast opening in Yucatan, or even to fill the urgent need of a permanent pastor over the flock at Gómez Farías. A supply of books was sent to Mérida, and our school books were introduced into some of the schools in that city, where the most unyielding fanaticism has no barrier but the most outspoken and scoffing infidelity, of the Bob Ingersoll type.

Yucatan differs from most of the other Mexican states in being the theatre of a war of races. In most parts of Mexico the wise plans of the Spanish viceroys had been instrumental in domesticating and civilizing the native races, and the absence of prejudice of race or color had led to an amalgamation of races and thus a unity of interest and relationship had bound the people together as one. In the peninsula of Yucatan it was otherwise. There was a bold, warlike and numerous tribe, called the Lacandones, who dwelt among the dense forests of the interior, and who seemed to have no desire to come to terms with the conquerors. They then believed,

DETAIL OF THE FACADE OF THE TEMPLE OF THE SUN AT UXMAL,

SHOWING THE ARCHITECTURAL PROGRESS OF THE ITZA KINGDOM.

For specimens of their Picture Writings see page 18.

and do even now, that it is possible to drive the
Europeans from America and blot out Christianity,
so as to restore the worship of Balaan Votan.

. Indeed it seems probable that they had already
blotted out a preceding civilization ere the Spanish
conquerors landed upon their arid soil. Strange ruins
abound in many places, which some antiquarians
suppose to be those of Itzalana, ruined by these
barbarian hordes not long before the conquest, whilst
others would have them as old as the pyramids of
Egypt or even older. Whatever be the date, it is
evident that in the architectural details, and
especially in sculpture they were far ahead of either
the Aztecs or the Incas, and not far behind the
Egyptians. We shall probably never have an authentic
history of their greatness, nor a correct idea of their
fall.

Whether that civilization was overthrown by the
Lacandones or not, one thing is certain, that the
existing civilization has more than once been in
imminent peril, and they have made the stronghold
of Merida tremble at their approach. The frontier
towns are often surprised at the dead of night by an
attack from these sons of the forest, and the firing
of rockets from the municipal building soon gathers
the people to defend their homes from the wild men
of the desert. Supplying themselves with arms and
ammunition from the British trading posts iu Balize
they are more formidable than the Sioux of our
northern frontier, whilst they at times become allies
of the frontier towns of Vera Paz in Guatemala,
which is the Republic of Central America which has
the strongest antipathies against the Mexican
government.

The thinking men of Mérida, and especially some
of her literary leaders having heard of the noble work
of the Society of Friends in conciliating the Indians
of North America, not only in the settlement of

J

Pennsylvania, but on the frontier during the administration of President Grant, were hoping that some such affort would be made in Yucatan.

We did not think best to send Luciano to Yucatan, and no foreign laborer was ready to enter that field, and as yet no Protestant mission is organized there, and the wild men of Chan Santa Cruz are still the dread of the frontier settlers of Yucatan and Campeachy.

# CHAPTER XIX.

BUILDING OF FRIENDS' MISSION CHAPEL. CONTINUED ILL HEALTH OF ANGELITA. OPENING OF THE NEW PLACE OF WORSHIP. REMOVAL TO GÓMEZ FARÍAS.

THE fall of 1879 was a memorable one in the history of the Friends' Mexican Mission because the building of a place of worship on one of the public squares changed greatly the sphere of action of the mission. A lot had been purchased a year previous on Plaza de la Libertad, and after many unexpected delays the work was begun in November of that year.

All our work was then removed to that square, and as nearly all our members resided in that vicinity the attendence became more regular than before.

Yet very many who saw those preparations, and who had desired to see the building completed, were to be laid away in their graves ere it was finished and opened for public worship.

The aged Petra Garcia de Mendez who had so often come to meeting reclining on a staff, bent with over ninety years of toil, was taken suddenly ill, and after lingering several days died in perfect trust and hope of salvation. The night before her death, after Luciano had read the Scriptures and prayed with her, Angelita began singing that beautiful hymn:—"Oh Sing to me of Heaven,"—and

131

the dying Christian joined her voice, weak indeed, but joyful, in singing of that land of unalloyed rest for the weary, where she had so earnestly desired to obtain an entrance through Christ her Savior.

The following day speech failed her but her face beamed with hope, and she gently passed away. Her real age was not known, though she had seen Matamoros grow from an insignificant ranch to a populous city. In evidence before the court she testified that in 1811, when the first war of Independence broke out, she was married and mother of three children; and thus she must have seen the scorching heat of well nigh a hundred summers. We had feared that so aged a convert would in second child-hood return to Romanism, but her death and that of an aged man about the same time showed the keeping power of Jesus even to those converted in the decline of life.

The next to follow was Patricia Arriaga de Cardona, a woman of dark Indian cast and in the meridian of life. Her husband had joined us some time before her conversion and had been quite useful in drawing others to attend our meeting, but had now fallen into sin, and had been disowned for adultery.

This resulted in their separation and the division of their children, and the heart-broken mother had to struggle for a living. Lung disease had set in and she was nearing the grave. One evening they sent for me but I was absent as was also Luciano, and on reaching home I hastened to the place, Angelita was there and had just read a selection from the Scriptures and had knelt in prayer. The woman's husband had come in bitter penitence and asked her forgiveness and was holding her emaciated form in his arms. She said that her own peace with God had been clouded, but she had sought forgiveness and could now rest on the promises of her Savior. Some of those sweet hymns so consoling to the dying believer were sung as she gently passed away, a sinner saved by grace, through faith in Christ.

Cecilio Chavez had long been a faithful elder in the service of the church and we had hoped he would long remain to cheer and aid us. Lung disease now hastily called him away. In his last walk he saw the trench dug for the foundation of the building, but a severe norther had aggravated the disease and he died suddenly yet trusting in Christ his Redeemer. One child had preceded him and another followed in a few weeks.

Julian Mireles had been convinced of the errors of Romanism by reading the Bible, one of the earliest circulated here, which came into his possession eighteen years before our arrival. It was issued by the American Bible Society though of Scio's version, from the Vulgate, without notes, so that he was one of the first fruits of Bible colportage in this country. He had been an elder several times in our Mission Church, elders being appointed at first every six months; and hoped to see the Mission Chapel opened for public worship. He was also smitten with the terrible disease which is so fatal in this severe climate, and the last time he visited the place the walls had reached the level of the windows. The funeral services took place in the Cemetery within the city walls, the only time I had preached there except at the grave of the little infant of Luciano and Angelita.

Strange as it may seem Angelita lingered along with slight fluctuations, through usually able to attend meetings. She often prayed that she might be spared to see the building completed, and her prayer was granted. She was able to be present and notwithstanding the brisk rain see the building crowded with people. The occasion will long be remembered, the rejoicing of the members and the earnest preaching impressed many hearts, and some who were there for the first time out of curiosity, afterwards were added to the fold.

The physicians had used every effort of medical science to save the life of Angelita and they now considered her case hopeless. A journey to the mountains offered a slight hope, and as we very anxious to gather those who were awakened at Gómez Farías during my visit and a year later by a brief tarriance there of one month by Luciano Mascorro, they were encouraged to go to that distant field. Efforts were made to make Angelita as comfortable as possible during the long overland journey, which was to be accomplished in an ambulance.

Never can we forget the beautiful day of her departure from this city. A solemn parting meeting was held at their residence, as several members, and among them her most intimate bosom friend, Gulielma, could not accompany her outside the city gate.

Whatever may have been the misgivings of those who were present, Angelita had high hopes of a recovery and was more cheerful than we had expected, as she had to bid farewell to her mother, sister and brother, whilst to the members who had been brought to Christ through her influence she was even more tenderly attached.

Many of these accompanied her outside the city walls to the grassy plains where the ambulance was waiting for the custom passes to be signed. Of this number no one attracted more attention than our Canadian co-laborer, W. A. Walls, who used every endeavor to make himself understood by Angelita, who told him that she desired to recover in order to work for Christ in the public ministry of the Gospel.

After a long and interesting parting interview they pursued their journey and we returned to our homes, earnestly desiring but hardly venturing to hope for the fulfillment of this sanguine wish of Angelita.

She suffered considerably from the fatigue inseparable from an overland journey of three hundred miles, to Victoria, capital of the State of Tamaulipas, where they spent a few weeks in order to rest and recruit,

ere proceeding to their final destination at Gómez
Farías. She was greatly interested by the change of
scenery, from the dead uniformity of the plains of
northern Tamaulipas, to the giant folds of the Sierra
Madre, and her tarriance in the most beautiful city of
the state was temporarily helpful to her. She was
cheered by the view of innumerable orange orchards,
and by the beautiful *alameda* or park on the outskirts
of the city, the street leading to which is lined with
sycamores, which are watered constantly by the
strongest channels of the irrigating works, which
distribute the water of the river San Márcos to the
orange orchards of the city, and the corn and cane-
fields of the surounding plains.

VICTORIA. (Mexico.)

It is difficult to obtain a view of the city of Victoria,
as its buildings are hidden by the dense shade of its
orange groves, but these make it look so green and
refreshing as to attract the traveller to its bosom,
whilst the bold outline of the Sierra Madre to the
westward, with the Sierra of San Cárlos to the
northward, and a series of isolated hills to the east-
ward, present a striking contrast to the unvarying
uniformity of the surroundings of most of the other
cities of Tamaulipas. The Presbyterian Mission had

been but recently established, but even there they found work to do for Christ during their tarriance.

Arrangements were finally perfected for their journey from Victoria to Gómez Farías, which was to be accomplished on horseback, by mule paths leading between the folds of the mountains, and with one or two pack animals for their baggage. The journey proved more fatiguing than they had anticipated as it rained constantly and they were often detained by flooded streams, having to spend a few days in some ranches by the wayside until the streams could be crossed. Thus a journey which in good weather could be accomplished in less than three days occupied nine, and the already delicate health of Angelita was severely tried by the exposure, and the beginning of their mission work was interrupted by her cough, thus her husband was unable to do much pastoral work from the necessity of constant attention at her bedside.

Meetings were kept up every Sabbath in the village chapel, which was kindly furnished by the authorities, who were favorable to the mission, and every night a Bible Class was kept up at their house. About a month later the believers were organized into a church, by the admission of sixteen members, and thus permanent work was organized, the nucleus of a now flourishing mission church, among the banana groves of Gómez Farías.

Luciano was kept at home so strictly by the illness of Angelita that we received no news from him for several months, there being no post-office in the village, and the facilities of communication were interrupted by the rainy season in the mountains.

Our anxiety about them induced us to send W. A. Walls to that village to learn their fate. The circumstances connected with this wonderful journey, and his narrow escape from imminent perils must form part of another chapter, as events at Matamoros of great moment to the future of the mission must claim our attention, for whilst they were wandering among the flooded streams of the Sierra Madre, the city of Matamoros had been nearly swept away by a terrific hurricane and its attendant inundation, news of which reached our Friends in their mountain home and awakened their anxiety about the dear ones they had left behind them.

Mexican Fruits. The Pomegranate.

FRIENDS' MEETING HOUSE MATAMOROS, MEXICO.
The day following the hurricane of 1880.

# CHAPTER XX.

UNEXPECTED and thrilling events now crowded upon the mission in such quick succession that our faith, accustomed to sudden and severe provings, was tried to the uttermost. But a little over a month after the departure of Luciano and Angelita for Gómez Farías, and just as the city was trembling with anxiety at a threatening inundation, one of those terrible Gulf hurricanes, so dreaded upon this coast, broke with unrelenting force upon the city, spreading desolation and distress upon every hand.

Never can the terrific scenes of that dark night be effaced from memory, and although vivid in our recollection, how much more so must it have been to those houseless amid the maddening fury of the storm, clinging to the ruins of their homes, who passed the night in the open air, unprotected from the piercing blast.

The dreadful hurricanes of 1867 and 1874 were still fresh in the memory of many of the citizens, and the ruins they left were still to be seen in many parts of the city, and whilst more damage was done to costly edifices in 1867, and that of 1874 lasted 72 hours, and was therefore more tedious, the hurricane of August 13th, 1880 fell with more force upon the working class, and the morning of the 14th, dawned upon the ruins of 1615 houses, mostly belonging to the poorer class of residents.

During all day of the 13th, the police force was busy in gathering the poor people from those shanties which seemed likely to fall, and some buildings near us fell during the afternoon, yet the greater part of the destruction took place between sundown and midnight, when there was a lull, followed by the dreaded south wind. One of our members brought his wife, with her new-born child, to take refuge in our house, and to satisfy her as well as to ascertain how our neighbors had fared, accompanied by W. A. Walls I made a tour around Liberty Square, finding the house of our friend still standing, though five buildings on the south side of the square, between our own and the store of I. Portilla had been blown to pieces, and the fragments distributed indiscriminately. The roof of a carriage shop adjoining our residence had been blown over our sitting room, throwing down some bricks from the parapet wall, and then striking our kitchen had thrown down about half of the gable, our school building was demolished, and the yard filled with fragments of neighboring buildings. During the whole storm both myself and Bro. Walls were busily occupied in bailing out the water which the wind was forcing under our north doors, and threatening us with an inundation. It is note-worthy that after having been a sufferer from rheumatism for some months, and even during the first part of the storm, I was forced to walk about barefoot, and often in several inches of water for about nine hours, and suffered no inconvenience, nor did the disease reappear.

One of the most interesting visits during that memorable night was to the residence of our friend and fellow-laborer Julio Gonzalez Gea, for on visiting our meeting house which had suffered considerably, we passed over the ruins of fences and shanties to his house, and seeing a light inside we knocked. We found his children asleep, and the Bible lay open upon the table, where during the force of the storm he had been reading the Psalms of David and engaged in earnest prayer for his fellow-beings. We saw him in an hour when all gloss was cast aside, but he was relying upon the promises of God. We never afterwards doubted the sincerity of his faith in Christ.

Many of our members had lost their houses, and were suffering for the necessaries of life, and we obtained a loan from a merchant to supply their wants, which was replaced by donations from Friends in the United States and England. However it was several weeks ere we had any mail facilities, the railroad from Brownsville to the coast was destroyed so that vessels could not discharge their freight, and we had to do what seemed best and leave the consequences with our Lord.

We may here remark that before it was possible for us to send either a telegram or a letter to Richmond, the Secretary of the Foreign Mission Committee, Timothy Harrison, had sent all the funds at their disposal for immediate use in the emergency.

Collections were taken among the wealthy to aid the poor and as our Mexican telegraph lines were not destroyed, the news of our disaster stirred the whole republic, and funds were speedily gathered to relieve the sufferers.

Nearly one third of the houses having been destroyed and one third of the town being still inundated, the poor people were lodged in the school and municipal buildings as well as in those houses which were unoccupied at the time, which were seized by the authorities for that purpose.

The small-pox, which had become a constant
resident of the suburbs, now broke out with relent-
less fury in the central part of the city, no reliable
vaccine matter was to be had, and before our mails
were re-established so that it could reach us, the
disease had invaded nearly every ward of the city,
and more then 500 persons had fallen victims to the
scourge, among them several of our flock.

Whilst this dark cloud was gathering over us, our
anxiety about Luciano and Angelita was daily
increasing, overland travel was greatly interrupted
by the inundation, which had flooded the whole
country and communication by sea with Tampico
was equally impracticable.

It was however decided that W. A. Walls should
make the attempt to reach them and it was not until
after his ticket was purchased by the coast line of
Steamers that we found that no carriage driver would
attempt the journey. We finally engaged a cartman
who left the city at 10 P. M. became bogged in the
lagoon and after swimming about for hours in search
of a practicable route across the lagoon, reached our
house in his defeat at 4 on the following morning.

Friend Walls ate breakfast and retired to rest
after his exposure during the night, when our energetic book agent, Antonio Ramirez had two cartmen
with three strong mules ready to take the risk of
placing our friend in a certainty of reaching Bagdad.

They reached at last a lagoon five miles across,
into which they drove until our friends were standing up to their knees in water, the cart wheels being
entirely submerged and it was evident that they could
go no further. Fortunately they saw a boat which
was repairing the telegraph line across the lagoon, to
which they made signals of distress and our Friend
was taken on board and on their return for the
night he was taken to Bagdad. The steamer arrived
next day, but a norther was blowing so that she

could not communicate with the shore, thus Friend Walls was obliged to return, which he did in company with some military officers, having to help row the boat against the current of the lagoon for about ten miles. On landing he hired a horse for his return journey, and a plan to rob him appears to have been frustrated by his meeting Antonio Ramirez, whom we had sent for him, ere his pursuers had overtaken him.

This unfortunate journey from Matamoros to Bagdad and return, a total of about sixty miles travel, had cost us $40. at a time when money was scarce, and for a few hours we thought any further effort undesirable.

However we learned that a cart from Victoria was to return empty, and it seemed possible for them to conduct him safely thus far, and a Presbyterian Mission having been established there we could have him safely acompanied to Gómez Farías. They offered him a passage for twelve dollars, which was accepted, and finaly we decided to send Manuel brother of Angelita, not only to cheer her, but to save him from the epidemic.

They reached their destination safely in about two weeks, and found Angelita alone, as Luciano had come to Victoria to mail letters, by another route, and did not reach home for a day or two after our Friend's arrival. However a Bible Class was kept up by Angelita in his absence, thought she was confined to her bed most of the time, and was evidently nearing the grave, she had however been actively engaged in persuading the people to abandon the worship of stocks and stones, and worship God in spirit and in truth. Writing at this time for "El Ramo de Olivo" she gives the following account of the benighted condition of the people among whom she was laboring, and whom she was striving to lead to Christ.

"Last year, in what are called the holy days, (or Lent,) notice was spread abroad that in one of the ranches near this village a

Virgin had appeared in the shade of a green lemon tree, that God, beholding the wickedness of men, (said the precursor of the Virgin, a girl of fifteen summers,) had sent that image to let the world know that if the people did not do penance, God would make an end of mankind. So soon as this notice spread among the ranches, the females of this and other villages gathered in great numbers to adore the Virgin, and from a certain distance they walked on their knees with lighted candles in their hands to the trunk of the lemon tree, where they beheld a small round stone surrounded by artificial flowers, which the ignorance and fanaticism of the people had converted into an image of the Virgin of Guadalupe, although in reality it was nothing more than one of the many beautiful stones to be found in the bed of our streams, adorned by seams of varied color.

"Not women alone, on this occasion, but also men noted in these parts for their learning, reverently approached the lemon tree on their knees to worship the image, repeated their prayers and sang hymns to the Virgin. No true picture of the Virgin was to be seen, even when these pious people looked earnestly and wiping their eyes looked again. Although some declared that they saw it, the greater part went away as they came, having seen no more than a stone rounded by the action of water in a mountain stream, 'Your many sins prevent your seeing it,' said a man whose fanaticism made him see the invisible, to a man of considerable intelligence who had failed to see the likeness. 'It may be so,' replied the man weeping with hopelessness for his many sins. The penitent went back to the starting point and again upon his knees traversed the penitential space and reverently bowed and worshipped the stone, and then looking closely failed to perceive the likeness, and returned again, hoping that the sharp stones which were cutting his knees would make God merciful to the penitent sinner, when all pain would be forgotten in the joy of beholding face to face the immaculate Virgin. But all his tears were in vain.

"Oh church of Rome! why dost thou call thyself the church of Christ, whilst teaching a way of salvation which he taught not! Why dost thou not teach that Jesus of Nazareth is the Way, the Truth and the Life, and that whosoever believeth in him hath pardon and salvation?

"But to return to my narrative. The pain caused by his wounds induced our penitent to return home and apply a remedy. His wife asked him what he knew about the Virgin, and he replied that it was a fable invented to deceive the credulous, and that notwithstanding having skinned his knees he had seen nothing.

"'You had better not be too hasty," replied his wife, but ere many weeks the greater part of the people became convinced that it was simply a stone which the hand of man had placed in the fork of the lemon tree.

"I cannot tell all which has been told me about this Virgin but in it we have another proof of what Christ in the Gospel tells us:— 'That the people loved darkness rather than Light.'

"I said at first that I intended to tell you about the work of the Lord in these parts, and you will be my companions in rejoicing that some of our countrymen are receiving the Gospel, or at least here they listen joyfully to the Word of God. I may say again that my soul is full of pleasure and rejoicing, as well as of gratitude to God, when I see many women who formerly believed in the worship of saints, and some of whom went to see the Virgin in the lemon tree, who now truly believe in Jesus Christ and his doctrine; and are ready to confess these before men; joining our church in Gómez Farías, and many more who constantly attend the meetings and listen reverently to the preaching of the Word.

"I can say the same of many men who are interested in the cause of Christ, and exhort their relatives and friends to search the Holy Scriptures, as the only fountain of divinely inspired teachings; and some of these are members and many more are believers in Christ.

"But whilst I rejoice for those sisters who have departed from error, believing in the only perfect Savior, and true Refuge of sinners, Christ Jesus, my heart is filled with mourning to see so many who persist in rebellion against God, worshipping, not our Redeemer, but dumb idols which are offensive to him, and which can be of no service to them in the final hour of life. But we must pray for such, and ask God to give them light and grace to know him of a truth.

"Lastly, dear sisters, I salute you with an embrace of love in Christ, asking God to bless you and fill you with his Spirit, that you may walk in the path which he has pointed out in his Gospel, in order that you may be prepared for the parting hour.

"As ever, you sister in the faith of Christ our Savior.

Angela Aguilan de Mascorro.

Villa de Llera, January 1st, 1881."

Our friend W. A. Walls returned to Matamoros, hastily and alone, to consult about the work, and when only about thirty miles from the city was surrounded by three highway robbers who endeavored to induce him to leave the main road and take a by path where they could carry out their design. A presentiment of danger induced him to refuse to accompany them and after threatening his life, and thereby receiving a strong lesson from his readiness to die if that were the Lord's will, they left him after

K

receiving from him half a dollar, although he told them that he had more, but needed it for his journey. It was very late one dark night about the middle of November that a loud call at our door summoned me from my studies, and recognizing the voice of Bro. Walls, I hastened to the door, when he said as I opened it, "Behold a certain man going from Jerusalem to Jehrico fell among thieves."

I did not ask an explanation but hastened to the yard to open the gate to admit his horse, and on dismounting he jovially said that he had a bag of oranges for Gulielma. I replied that she was in North Carolina, to which he paid no attention, and it was not until he had entered the house, and found me alone, that each became convinced that what had seemed joking was sober reality.

The giant strides of the epidemic and the impossibility of vaccination, as well as the constant danger of the contagion, since persons covered with the raw sores came daily to our doors to ask for some aid, or to fulfil some errand, put our only child, a boy of six weeks so constantly in danger, that Gulielma, with a mother's solicitude, determined to hasten her proposed visit to her parents, after an absence of ten years, and had already reached her destination.

At first we thought best for Bro. Walls to fill my place, to allow me to join my wife in her visit, but it was finally determined that he should return to the Southern Mission in company with Francisco Peña, who had recently begun preaching the Gospel, whilst it seemed advisable for Luciano and Angelita to retire to Llera where the houses were |better adapted to her comfort during the winter season so that early in December our friends were again traversing the state, and Bros. Walls and Peña were ministering to the church at Farías, and Luciano and Angelita were gathering a congregation in Llera.

Whilst Angelita lived in Farías, she stayed at the house of Antonia Rosas, whose father while personally friendly to her, was very much opposed to her religion.

He was a little deaf and used his deafness as a shield, always becoming quite unable to hear so soon as the subject of personal salvation was introduced. He slept in the kitchen in order not to be present at family prayer, a custom which he continued whilst Francisco Peña and W. A. Walls lived in the house. When the latter commenced teaching his grandchildren, the old man who was intelligent, although uneducated, was very anxious that the children should make progress in their studies, and to encourage them he listened to their accounts of what they had learned during the day. He thus heard many texts of Scripture, and as afterwards appeared learned several hymns by heart. During all these years since Angelita's visit, prayer was continually offered for his conversion. Bro. Gonzalez was surprised to learn that old Andrew had sent for him, and on reaching the house he was met with the inquiry; —"What must I do to be saved." He explained to him the work of Christ as our Savior. The aged penitent said;— "I know that is so," and repeated several conclusive texts which he had learned from the children.

He lived about six months after his conversion. When he accepted Christ, he did so so fully that he never asked for the images of saints, the crosses and medals in which he formerly trusted, and was very thankful to be saved from dying in idolatry.

Ere closing this chapter it may be well to give a further insight into the singular experience of Bro. Walls with the Mexican highwaymen, which we do in his own words as published at the time in the "Christian Worker"

We had already warned him of the danger of travelling alone and certainly should have protested most earnestly against it, but his decision was made over four hundred miles away and carried out without our consent.

"Before reaching Matamoros I got a lesson which would have convinced the sturdiest of doubters. On Tuesday started at 3 o'clock in the morning, partly because the rain made my ebony bush an uncomfortable roof, and partly because a seventy mile trip lay between my bedroom and Matamoros. About 9 in the morning I was overtaken by three horsemen, all on good horses, but as we were within sight of a farm they simply passed the usual 'Buenos dias, señor,' and rode on to the house. I did not like their appearance, but as I had no business at the farm I rode quietly past. When about a mile beyond I was again over-taken by the same company, and they now proposed that we should journey to Matamoros together. Consenting to the arrange-ment, one of them went immediately in front and the others one at each side of my horse.

"As this order of march was a little suspicious, I turned my beast suddenly, so as to be at the side of the road, and saw that one of my companions had a pistol in his hand, which he put out of sight as quickly as possible, and supposed it had escaped observation. I now knew the character of my companions, and could simply put up a fervent petition to our Father for protec-tion. The leader of the company offered to show me a shorter road to Matamoros, and proposed that we should leave the high-way to find this short cut. When I declined this obliging offer, which was intended to draw me into the chapparal, where the buzzards would probably be the only discoverers of the body, he threw off his mask of pretended kindness, and pointing his pistol at my head, threatened me with instant death if I did not follow the foremost of the company. As it seemed like leaving the path of duty, I refused to leave the only place in which I had a right to expect God's protection. The front man now seized my horse's halter and attempted to lead him away from the road. I at once dismounted and with a jerk freed the rope from his grasp.

"'Knives, men,' said the captain, and two knives, each over a foot long, were held threateningly over my breast. Then the captain a second time ordered me, on pain of immediate death, to accompany them to the northward. The reply was, 'You may kill me if you will, it makes no difference to me; thanks to God I am ready, but this is my road, and from here I will not go.' 'Are you prepared?' 'Yes.' The idea seemed a novel one, and the knives disappeared, though the pistol, with its five barrels all charged, still remained pointed at my face. I then asked who they were, and where they lived, and was told that they were

'Gentlemen of St. John,' and lived under the moon. He now demanded my money. I gave him a fifty-cent piece which I had in my pocket, not caring to show my purse, which contained about eight dollars—more than I could afford to lose. He said:—'It is very little; have you no more?' 'Yes, but I need the rest,' which was quite true.

He again asked for it, but in a somewhat doubtful tone, as if he expected to be refused, and it seemed to me that I need make no further sacrifice, so I told him that I could spare the half-dollar, but no more. 'Vamos, let us be off,' he said to his fellow bandits, and they galloped on at a lively rate.

"Returning thanks to God, who had so wonderfully delivered me from the hands of these highwaymen, I remounted and at a slower pace followed. Certainly it is not usual for the Mexican 'road agents' to let their victim escape with his life, much less to carry his money out of their hands. I can only praise God, who, in the moment of peril, kept my mind perfectly quiet. When I refused to leave the road I expected to receive a shot instantly, and as the mind works with more than lightning rapidity the thought of past occupations, apparently important once, but now, when face to face with eternity, utterly trivial, filled me with shame for wasted opportunities; at the same time I had an unutterable gladness at the thought that sudden death was sudden glory, that to leave this earth was only to leave earthly friends for the presence of Him who is dearer than all other friends.

"While regretting the misspent time and lost opportunities, I felt great calmness from the knowledge that through the blood of Christ I was accepted, and was enabled to say in my heart, 'O Lord! deliver Thy servant in Thine own way, by life for Thy service on earth, or by death for Thy praise in heaven.'

"I have often thought, and now know, that the mind can carry on several operations at the same time. While meditating on my past life, and rejoicing that the question of salvation was settled, I was also wondering at the same instant how it feels to be shot, and whether he intended to fire at the head or the heart, whether a second shot would be necessary, and what Mr. Purdie would say when he heard of it. Also I thought of the pain which the news would give at home, all apparently in an instant. One idea, amusing from its triviality, kept coming up, certainly without any effort of mine suddenly presented itself, 'Well, Mrs. Purdie will never get her oranges.' While so many other important questions were occupying my attention, this was certainly an odd notion for that moment. I also remember counting repeatedly the five barrels of the pistol, and even noted the carving of the handle with a singular curiosity."

# CHAPTER XXI.

PREPARATIONS FOR MY ABSENCE. ENCARNACION GON-
ZALEZ AND WIFE JOIN OUR MISSION, AND ARE SENT
TO GÓMEZ FARÍAS. LUCIANO AND ANGELITA RETURN
TO MATAMOROS. HER DEATH. EULOGY WRITTEN BY
CALIXTO LARA. CONCLUDING REMARKS.

IT now seemed evident that in order to permit my
absence it would be necessary for Luciano to
be stationed at Matamoros, and all hopes of any
improvement in the health of Angelita having
been abandoned it was thought best for them to
return. The English correspondence of the Mission
would require the presence of W. A. Walls, whilst
Francisco Peña was but just beginning to labor in
the public ministry, and his wife being a firm Roman
Catholic he could not well be located at the head of
the Southern Mission, whilst Julio Gonzalez Gea was
even younger in the ministry and his family would
greatly increase the expense of his transfer.

Just at this needy hour Encarnacion Gonzalez, and
elder of the Presbyterian church, who had long felt
colled to work of the ministry, requested for a transfer to our church, as his age was an obstacle to his
studying for the ministry in a church requiring a
knowledge of the dead languages, and he had but a
limited education in his own. He was however a
constant student of the Scriptures and a most conscientious and devout Christian. This seemed providential at that juncture, and as my health seemed to
require it, Bro. Walls returned during the latter part
of February 1881, and arrangments were made for

sending Encarnacion Gonzalez and wife to the Southern Mission, a carriage was purchased, which left Matamoros on the day following my departure for North Carolina.

They reached Llera in nine days, and as soon as they had their baggage transferred to Gómez Farías, our horses being used for pack animals, Luciano and Angelita began their toilsome return journey, being acompanied by Francisco Peña.

Ten leagues from Victoria one wheel of the carriage gave way, and abandoning it there, they proceded on horseback to Victoria, where another vehicle was procured and in seven days' travel they reached Matamoros.

Angelita was greatly emaciated, indeed they feared she would not reach her destination, but she ardently desired to see her mother and sister and to die among those persons to whom she was so clohely bound in church fellowship; and this wish was granted her.

It is true that the surroundings at the mission rooms still seemed lovely to her, but the very persons to whom she was most closely bound in fellowship, and of whose home she had been for several years an inmate were absent, and the little babe she so much desired to take in her arms ere called to another world, was more than a thousand miles away, yet the house was filled by the brethren who flocked to see her and to listen to the earnest exhortations from her dying lips.

She only survived three days after her arrival, and was often engaged in helping sing those hymms which are so full of consolation for the dying Christian, and as death was closing upon her she aided her husband in singing the 136th Psalm, so full of praise to God for his many mercies.

The funeral, upon the following day, was attended by an immense number of people, not only members of the two mission churches, but many friends of the deceased and those who had become intimate friends of Luciano for his literary attainments, and including some of the most wealthy and influential citizens.

She was buried in the cemetery outside the city walls, where most of our deceased members lie, a very numerous company following the corpse to the grave.

She died just as she seemed prepared for the true service of life, cut short ere reaching the meridian of her days mourned by all who knew her, and the mission church realized that the dear young woman who had been called away at but twenty one years of age had been to them a mother in Israel.

They had heard her sweet voice sing the praises of her Lord, when a robust maiden of sixteen years, and had watched her growth in grace and usefulness, until the hand of disease had left but a physical ruin, which had now been removed for ever from this scene of toil and suffering.

Perhaps no better words can be found to express the feelings of our members than those of Calixto Lara, formerly our colporteur, in the following eulogy which was published in "El Ramo de Olivo" and which shows not only how a Mexican feels but how he can express those feelings.

"With deep pain I take the pen to consecrate a few lines to the memory of this sister in the common faith, who descended to the grave on the 28th of March.

"Death, perennial fountain of tears and sighs, indefatigable worker of oblivion, has deprived us of seeing henceforth a sister in Christ, and an active member of his militant church in this world of trials and sufferings.

"It is but a little while since we saw her solicitously exhorting the other members to follow with a firm step the narrow and rugged road to the celestial city, and exhorting those living in the darkness of error and superstition to repentance of their sins and to the observance of the pure maxims of the Gospel, and to faith in the Redeemer of the world whose blood cleanseth us from all sin.

"A little while ago we saw her with joyful and smiling countenance give bread to the hungry, and console and assist those who were suffering on the bed of pain. An obedient daughter, a loving and amiable sister, a faithful wife, a sincere and well-wishing friend. Her love for good was invincible, and she never ceded before the obstacles which constantly present themselves to impede and make difficult the exercise of this sublime virtue.

"In vain my words essay to analyze, much less express the just encomium due to the virtues of a person to whom I was bound by the cords of respect and gratitude; this is a task worthy of more expert pens and greater intelligence; but it is pleasing to portray even though imperfectly the gifts with which Providence had endowed this tender flower, wilted in the morning of life.

"Neither the muteness of the sepulchre, nor the darkness of the tomb, are sufficient to vail the splendid glories of great souls; no, their record remains engraved in indelible characters in the hearts of the survivors, which neither time nor evil-speaking can becloud. Her genius leaps across the bottomless pit of oblivion where generations are buried, and centuries will roll by respecting her name and memory.

"She has fulfilled faithfully her mission in this transitory world, bequeathing us an example which should be imitated by all true Christians.

"Her body, inert matter which served as a tabernacle for her spirit, has returned to dust, because it was formed of dust, but her soul, where is it? It is in the presence of her Savior, enjoying the reward of her work, clothed in the white robes of purity and incorruptibility and her forehead encircled with the unfading crown of victory, a conqueror by faith in the merits of the Son of Man. Blessed are the dead who die in the Lord."—C. LARA.

This death scene inspired the following remarks on the death bed of a Christian, which with the initials of the bereaved husband appeared in the same number of "El Ramo de Olivo."

"How sweet, how serene and happy is the death of the faithful believer in the Lord Jesus!

"Happy instant, long wished for moment, when that which is most in the human being, and which makes it superior to the brute creation, the soul, casting off its fleshly clothing, not in its own will, but in virtue of the divine will, flies rapidly to the place of eternal rest, to reunite with those who like her * have waited and watched for the coming of him who said. Watch then, for ye know not the hour when your Lord cometh. Mat. 24:42.

* "Alma" soul is feminine, and he evidently intends to be understood as speaking of the death of Angelita.

"In her looks, in her words are reproduced felicity, peace and contentment. The calmness with which she submits to the sharpest pains, shows us that in her soul a supernatural power is working; and this teaches and incites to bless the fountain of every good and perfect gift.

"Oh Sublime Gospel! of a truth thou art the Good News, the consoling message of God to humanity."—L. M.

The news of the death of Angelita reached the writer, just as he was entering a Bible School Conference at Back Creek, N. C. where the telegram was read and a sermon appropriate to so solemn an occasion was preached by Rufus P. King, and will long be remembered by all who were privileged to be present, giving a just tribute to the dear departed Christian, and an exhortation to improve the brief years of our life in the service of Jesus.

# CHAPTER XXII.

## SKETCH OF THE MISSION FROM THE DEATH OF ANGELITA TO THE PRESENT TIME.

MANY changes have taken place in the Friends' Mexican Mission since the death of this dear sister. We returned to Matamoros in the latter part of August 1881, and resumed charge of the work. The sister of Angelita was married to our Friend W. A. Walls on the 29th of the same month, and they were stationed at Escandon where they labored for two years under the Foreign Mission Committee of Ohio Yearly Meeting.

In April 1882 the meeting under charge of José María Garza at Cadereita Jimenez, which had been organized as a Congregationalist Mission some years before, and where several desired liberty of conscience in regard to Baptism, which some deemed as not required of them, accepting it only in a spiritual sense, was recognized by our meeting at Matamoros as a sister church and a part of our Mission, though receiving no pecuniary support except books. Our Friend Garza was placed in charge of the prisoners in the city jail where a night school was started for the prisoners and he had good success in evangelistic work among them, having been instrumental in the conversion of several persons who had been hardened in crime.

155

Branch meetings have been held at San Francisco de Apodaca and several other towns near there, either by our Friend José María Garza or by some of the members of his congregation who have felt called to public labor for Christ.

The work at San Fernando was resumed in the Spring of 1882 by Julio Gonzalez Gea, who opened a Day School. For three months after announcing his school no children came, but as fear began to diminish a few boys were sent in. This developed into a school of thirty pupils who were daily taught many important Gospel Truths, and has resulted in the conversion of the second magistrate of the village, Santiago García Gonzalez, who has had charge of the Grammar classes in the school, though working voluntarily as an unpaid coadjutor. He feels called to the ministry and we trust will be a useful laborer in the near future. His sister Gertrudis G. de Uresti, has since been converted and has charge of a Girls' School at Mendez, an out-station of the San Fernando Mission, which is sustained by the Foreign Mission Committee of New York Yearly Meeting of Friends. Her school receives books free from our Publishing House at Matamoros, but a small stipend from parents sustains the teacher at present. Thus that station which gave so little promise when Luciano and Angelita were there, has given to the cause of Christ two able native laborers, who are ready to leave home and go forth in the Cause of their Redeemer.

The little gathering at Gómez Farías has grown to a large meeting of over 100 attenders, having among its members the most influential residents, and a nice meeting house, known as Mendenhall Chapel, built by Richard J, and Abby G. Mendenhall of Minneapolis, who sustain that mission and are planning further improvements.

Luciano was married to Virginia Washington, teacher of our Girls' School in December 1882, and they are now in charge of the new mission at Santa Bárbara, 45 miles from Gómez Farías, the cradle of the Mexican Reform movement of Father Lozano. The priest of that village had married a few weeks before they arrived, and is now using his influence in favor of the new Evangelical movement. A local Evangelical paper is issued every two weeks, and has an extensive circulation and influence in the whole Southern part of Tamaulipas. Luciano as Superintendant of the Southern Mission is busy organizing a circuit for stated meetings in several other villages of that section.

In April 1882 our mission was joined by Librado Ramirez, who had been connected with the Presbyterian Mission, and who was stationed at Soto la Marina in August 1883. The prospect of that being opened as a port for foreign commerce and becoming a Railroad centre led us to prefer that station, but the failure of this latter may lead to his transfer to some other point. The Women Friends of Western Yearly Meeting have sent Ora Osborne and Lillie Neiger of Danville Ind. to join him in the Mexican field.

The work at Matamoros has not been forgotten by those who watch over it, and although commercial depression has led to the emigration of more than one half of our members, including our most stable native elders, to other points, the attendance has not diminished and the Bible School is now, fall of 1884, in the most flourishing condition. The Girls' School being led by Julia L. Ballenger, who is sustained by Women Friends of Philadelphia, aided by Luisa Flores, a native teacher, who is sustained by Women Friends of Indiana Yearly Meeting. It is now developing into a Boarding School, with rich promise for the Mexican Church.

A Dorcas Society has been organized for clothing the needy, and in connection with it a weekly visit to all the families of its members, with Scripture reading and prayer at each house, which is developing the evangelistic effort of the female part of our meeting. Among the converts to Protestantism through these efforts is Librada Mascorro de Moreno, a sister of Luciano Mascorro and who had until then been a most resolute Catholic, even when one brother was a minister, and her mother and another brother members of Protestant churches.

Santos Rodriguez de Gonzalez, wife of our minister at Gómez Farías is an able female evangelist, nearly equal in zeal to Angelita, and Virginia W. de Mascorro gives promise of good service is the Cause of Christ, thus we trust God will continue to bless us with native female evangelists who like Phebe and Priscilla, Tryphena and Tryphosa, Persis and Lydia, may prove themselves worthy successors of that long list of female prophets and teachers, who have adorned the Gospel of our Lord and Savior with their holy lives and their eloquent words for Jesus.

Whilst the growth of evangelistic and school work has been thus enlarged, the publishing department has far outstepped them both. From month to month new calls for our religious books reach us from all parts of Mexico, Texas and New Mexico, from all of the Republics of Central America, from Cuba, Porto Rico and Santo Domingo [Hayti] as well as Colombia, Venezuela, Chili, the Argentine Republic and Uruguay in South America, and in all these we are supplying reading rooms and public libraries, and by means of our exchange papers bringing a direct influence on the public mind, and upholding the Gospel standard as the healing balm for individuals, families and nations, as it will be to all who receive it the power of God unto salvation.

These nations have drunk the cup of war to the dregs, have seen its devastating influence as well as its demoralizing tendency and many are longing for some token of permanent peace and moral and social progress.

The thinking minds are alive to many important questions and perhaps abler arguments against the death penalty, and against judicial oaths have never been produced than those wielded by the legislators of Spanish America. These are special reasons why the Society of Friends, which has long stood almost alone in upholding testimonies against these and kindred evils should tend a helping hand, to present these reforms not from a rationalistic point of view, but from a Gospel standpoint, not as the elimination of human reasoning, but as the teachings of God manifest in the flesh, as the Savior of the world.

The work has hardly begun, and there seems to be no limit to that which should be done *now* in these needy fields, fast ripening unto the harvest. The awakening now going on in the Society of Friends in regard to Foreign Missions is a token for good, and we trust that this little volume may contribute to foster that interest, not only in showing to those blessed with means the fruit of their efforts in the past and the opportunities of the future, but that it will be instrumental in fostering in others a willingness to give themselves to the Lord in these fields and with all the energies they possess consecrated wholly to his service, be ready to go forth trusting in Him who hath called them, and count it all joy to endure *hardness*, whether it be in encountering hardships or in suffering persecution for the furtherance of this blessed work.

Above all let us pray unto the Master of the vineyard, that he send forth more laborers into his vineyard, that he raise up many among the sons and daughters of Spanish America, who like the subject of our narrative, like the noble sons and daughters of Spain whoe sealed their testimony to Jesus with their lives in the Autos de Fé of Valladolid and Seville, may fulfill the injunction of the Apostle:—"I BESEECH YOU THEREFORE, BRETHREN, BY THE MERCIES OF GOD, THAT YE PRESENT YOUR BODIES A LIVING SAC-RIFICE, HOLY, ACCEPTABLE UNTO GOD, WHICH IS YOUR REASONABLE SERVICE." Rom. XII. 1.

## *THE END.*